The Secret Pony

Library and Archives Canada Cataloguing in Publication

White, Julie L., 1958-
 The secret pony / Julie L. White.

ISBN 1-55039-148-8

 I. Title.

PS8645.H58S42 2004   jC813'.6   C2004-904550-4

Sono Nis Press most gratefully acknowledges the support for our publishing
program provided by the government of Canada through the Book Publishing
Industry Development Program (BPIDP), the Canada Council for the Arts, and
the British Columbia Arts Council.

Cover and chapter illustration (detail of cover) by Joan Larson
Edited by Laura Peetoom
Cover and interior design by Jim Brennan

Published by
Sono Nis Press
Box 160
Winlaw, BC V0G 2J0

1-800-370-5228

books@sononis.com
www.sononis.com

Distributed in the U.S. by
Orca Book Publishers
Box 468
Custer, WA 98240-0468

1-800-210-5277

The Canada Council | Le Conseil des Arts
for the Arts | du Canada

Printed and bound in Canada.

The Secret Pony

Julie White

sononis PRESS WINLAW, BRITISH COLUMBIA

To my family,

Thanks for the encouragement and doing the chores
while I wrote "just one more sentence."

1

"Hey, what are you doing with that pony?"

Kirsty hurried across the soggy lawn, the bag of apples slapping against her legs. Lancelot stood with his front feet braced on the ramp of a rusting old horse trailer. His neck was stretched out, pulled tight by the cotton lead rope snapped to his halter. Kirsty could see a man inside the trailer tugging on the other end of the rope.

The pinto pony didn't budge. Suddenly, he gave a mighty heave and jerked the lead rope right out of the man's hands. He trotted off over the damp grass with the rope flapping around his legs.

"Whoa! Whoa now!" The man jumped off the trailer ramp and chased after Lancelot. The pony veered away and headed for the main road.

"Lancelot, come here," called Kirsty. She sucked her bottom lip and let out a piercing whistle.

Lancelot twisted his body around, changing direction in midstride. Catching sight of Kirsty, he whinnied.

She held out an apple. "Here boy, come on." The pony jogged up to her, holding his head sideways to keep from tripping on the dangling rope. He snatched the apple and gobbled it greedily, bunting her for more before he was even finished chewing.

The man stomped up and grabbed the lead rope.

"C'mon, you."

"Leave him alone!"

The man blinked at the young girl attached to the pony's halter, bright hazel eyes glaring, square chin held high. "Who are you?"

Kirsty ignored the question. "Where's Mr. Jensen? Does he know you have his pony?"

"What's the pony got to do with you?"

"I'm Kirsty Hagen. I live down the road and I've been looking after Lancelot." She held out another apple to the pinto pony. It really was the truth. Old Mr. Jensen hadn't been home for nearly three days. After the first day, when Kirsty realized no one was caring for the pony she'd named Lancelot, she'd taken it upon herself to throw him a flake or two of the coarse grass hay from the shed beside his dirt corral. The hay had run out yesterday morning. Since then she'd brought food from home, everything she thought a pony would possibly eat – oatmeal, brown bread, carrots, and apples.

"Well, you won't have to bother with him much longer. He's going to the auction."

"What? Does Mr. Jensen know what you're doing? Did he say you could sell his pony?"

"Uncle's in the hospital. He's got cancer."

"Oh. Is he going to be all right?"

The nephew shook his head. "Probably not."

Kirsty stared at him, wanting to ask exactly what "probably not" meant and not daring in case it was the worst. "He said I could ride his pony when the snow melted. It's been gone for weeks now."

"Sorry, but the situation's changed, kid. Uncle Jensen asked me to take care of things here. I've got no place for a pony, so he's got to be sold." The man sighed, running his hand down Lancelot's skinny neck. "You poor old bag of bones. We'll be lucky to get a hundred bucks for you."

"One hundred dollars? Is that all he's worth?"

The man shrugged. "Might bring more, but I doubt it."

Impetuously, Kirsty blurted out the first thought in her head. "I've got a hundred dollars. I could buy him."

"Sure you could, if your folks say it's okay. Better ask them quick because I've got to know right away."

Kirsty paused. She wanted this pony more than anything. Quickly she made her decision. "Can I use the phone to call my mom at work?"

"My cell phone's in the truck. You can call her on that."

"Community Services." Darwin's voice sounded faraway on the tiny cell phone. He was the other social worker at Mom's office.

"Darwin, it's me. Is Mom there?"

"Hello, Me. No, Kirsty, she's gone to a meeting in Vernon. She should be back soon."

"But I've got to talk to her right away! It's really important."

"Kirsty, are you all right? Is there some kind of trouble?"

"No, nothing like that. I just really need to ask her something."

"Well, I'll tell her to call you the moment she gets in the door."

Kirsty thanked Darwin and hung up. Mr. Jensen's nephew slapped the end of the lead rope against his jeans while Lancelot cropped at the dried weeds next to the tool shed. "Well, what's the word?"

"She's at a meeting right now."

"Too bad. Okay, Spot, let's get you on that trailer."

"Wait! She's going to call back soon."

"Listen, I can't be hanging about here all afternoon."

"I know, I know. Look, I'll go home and get the money. I'll call my mom again. I won't be very long. Please, wait just a little bit longer."

"All right. I'll hold off another half-hour. I've got some stuff to pack up in the house anyway."

"Oh, thank you so much!" Kirsty hugged Lancelot's skinny neck. He nuzzled her brown ponytail, puffing hot air on her cheek.

"I'll give you my cell phone number. Tell your mom to phone me on it."

He jotted down the number on a scrap of paper. Kirsty stuffed it into her jeans pocket. She hugged Lancelot again and ran off.

She lived just three houses away from Mr. Jensen, but a couple of hayfields and a cow pasture in between meant they were just over a kilometre apart. When they moved to the North Okanagan last summer, Mom had promised they'd have a little farm with a garden, chickens, sheep, and a pony for Kirsty. She had been dreaming – again. After the divorce, when the house in Vancouver was sold and everything divided up, she could only afford a sagging, tin-roofed farmhouse on a rough, sloping half-acre near Armstrong.

Kirsty turned off the road and forced her aching legs up the dirt track that passed for a driveway. She stumbled up the steps of the veranda and dug the house key out of the crack under the window ledge. An elderly black Labrador barked as the kitchen door banged open.

"It's okay, Jet. Don't get up." The old dog thumped his thick tail and snuggled into his bed by the woodstove.

Kirsty kicked off her runners as she grabbed the phone. She punched in the numbers and took a couple of deep gulps of air to steady her breathing. "Darwin! Is she back yet?"

"Not yet, Kirsty, but she should be here any minute."

"Make sure she phones me right away, okay? Please?"

"Got it. Call Kirsty right away. Sure I can't help you?"

"No, Darwin, I've got to talk to my mom. Bye."

Kirsty dashed upstairs to her room. Diving under her bed, she dug out a cookie tin with a mare and foal pictured on the lid. *Thank you, Dad, for sending me money for my birthday.* She counted out one hundred dollars and shoved the tin back. Stuffing the money in her pocket, she clattered down the narrow stairs.

"Come on, come on." She paced the floor of the little kitchen, hopping back and forth over Jet's legs. Nearly twenty minutes had passed. Something must have gone wrong. What if the car had a flat tire? Or worse – what if it had broken down? Then her mother wouldn't be back at the office for hours. Kirsty couldn't wait much longer.

Mom *had* promised her a pony. Kirsty pulled out the slip of paper and dialed the number on it quickly.

"Hello!"

Kirsty deepened her voice. "This is Linda Hagen. I'm phoning to say it's all right for my daughter to buy the pony."

"Oh, sure. Don't you want to have a look at him?"

"Huh?"

"The pony. Don't you want to see what your kid's getting?"

"Umm, well, I'm at work right now. Kirsty knows what she wants. . . and it's her money. Just let her have the pony."

"All right then. That's fine by me. What name do you want on the bill of sale?"

Bill of sale? Things were getting pretty serious. Kirsty swallowed to wet her suddenly dry throat. "Kirsty's name. Put that name on it."

After saying goodbye she carefully replaced the phone and sank into a chair. Jet laid his broad head on her knee.

"I've got a pony, Jet. A pony of my very own." Her heart pounded. She was actually getting a pony. "I've got to get back and pay for him."

She shoved her feet back into her runners and scooted out the door. *Oh boy. What was Mom going to say?*

"Good enough." Mr. Jensen's nephew passed Kirsty a slip of paper. She studied it, frowning. As far as she could make out from the cramped handwriting, it said she was now the owner of a twelve-year-old, fourteen-hand, black-and-white pinto pony. *We're the same age,* she thought.

"Are you sure you're allowed to do this? I mean, sell me Mr. Jensen's pony?" Lancelot sniffed at the paper in her hand and tried to nibble a corner. Kirsty gently batted his muzzle.

"I've got something called power of attorney. That means it's legal for me to sell Uncle's stuff for him. That includes the pony."

"But he knows about this, right? He won't be mad at me?"

"I'll tell him tonight when I go visit him in the hospital. He's been worried about the pony. He'll be happy to know he's got a good home."

Kirsty nodded. Lancelot was dozing in the weak March sun, one hip sagging. He was starting to shed his winter coat. She stroked his shoulder and her hand was covered in black and white hairs. *He's like a black-and-white checkerboard.* She pictured him sleek and plump, his mane and tail combed and silky.

"Aren't you going to take him home?"

"Huh? Oh, yeah, right now. Come on, Lancelot. We're going home."

She couldn't keep her eyes off the pony as he clopped along beside her. Somehow he seemed larger now that he was on the other end of the lead rope than he ever had in Mr. Jensen's corral. He shied away from a white Styrofoam cup lurking in the bushes, his chipped hooves just missing Kirsty's toes. She remembered to stiffen her arm and hold him well away from her, the way she'd been shown at riding camp.

It wasn't until they'd turned in at the driveway that Kirsty began to worry about where to put her new pony.

"I guess I could tie you to a tree, but you wouldn't be able to move around much. And what would you eat?"

That left the old chicken pen. She held her breath as Lancelot squeezed through the narrow gate. "Sorry about this, boy, but at least you've got some grass to eat in here." The pony yanked at the halter, trying to reach the blades of new grass poking through the dirt. Kirsty unbuckled the halter and slipped it off. Lancelot dived at the grass.

"I'll get you a bucket of water. Be right back."

She was scrubbing out a bucket at the kitchen sink when the phone rang.

"Kirsty!" It was Mom. "Are you all right? Is everything okay?"

"I'm fine, Mom."

"Oh, thank goodness. Darwin said you wanted me to call right away. He said it sounded urgent. I thought something had gone wrong."

"Mom, you worry too much. Where are you? Are you coming home soon?"

"I'm just leaving the office, sweetie. The meeting ran late. I'd planned to pick up the groceries, but maybe I should come right home."

"Get the groceries, Mom. I've got something to tell you, but it can wait until you get home. And there's nothing good to eat in this house."

"Well, if you're sure. I'll be home in an hour."

"Mom, don't worry so much."

"Hey, it's my job. See you soon."

"Get some more carrots, please. And oatmeal."

"You're on a real health food kick these days. Okay, sweetheart, see you soon."

"Bye, Mom."

After hanging up, Kirsty filled the bucket and lugged

it out to the chicken pen. Lancelot had grazed every single blade of grass.

"Don't you ever do anything but eat?"

He lipped the end of her brown ponytail, obviously still hungry.

"Okay, okay, I get the hint. I'll see what I can find."

Kirsty leafed through all her pony books and strained to recall everything she'd learned at riding camp about what to feed a pony. She poured the rest of the breakfast oatmeal and a whole box of corn flakes into a bucket and added chopped apples, carrots, bran, and chunks of brown bread. On top she drizzled most of a carton of molasses. The results didn't look very appetizing.

Lancelot sniffed the bucket suspiciously when she placed it in front of him.

"Sorry, boy, but it's the best I can come up with. And it's just for today, I promise. I'll get Mom to buy you some hay tomorrow."

She watched anxiously as Lancelot ate, praying he wouldn't get colic. All the books warned not to change a pony's diet suddenly. New foods had to be introduced slowly or else the pony could end up with a terrible stomach ache and possibly even die.

"But I have no choice, do I, Lancelot? I can't just let you go hungry."

She shivered. The sun was sinking behind the mountains. She huddled close to Lancelot's warmth, breathing in his sweet grassy scent.

Lancelot lifted his head. Kirsty listened. She could hear a low rumble growing louder. "That must be Mom's car."

She was right. The little car chugged up the steep drive. The engine cut and a door slammed.

"Mom! Over here!"

"Kirsty? Will you come here right now?"

"Uh-oh. She sounds grumpy. I'd better go see what she wants." She gave the pony another pat, just to remind herself he was real.

2

"Give me a hand packing in these groceries." Mom thrust a cardboard carton at Kirsty. She always insisted on boxes instead of plastic bags. Cardboard was easier to recycle.

"How was your meeting, Mom?" asked Kirsty, following her mother up the stairs to the veranda.

Mom shuddered, her cropped brown hair quivering. "Long and boring. I don't know how I stayed awake. You know, if anybody had told me this job involved so many meetings, I probably wouldn't have taken it."

Kirsty rested the box on the veranda railing. "Sure, Mom. You love your job."

Mom worked for the local community service organization. It coordinated many local social services, including the food bank for people who didn't have enough money to buy groceries. Mom's job didn't pay much money, as she often reminded Kirsty. "But at least I'm doing something that makes a difference."

That remark would be a dig at Kirsty's father. He'd gone back to school a few years earlier to become an accountant for a large company. "Can you imagine spending your day keeping track of nickels and dimes?" Mom would say, rolling her eyes. "How does that help make this world a better place, I'd like to know."

Mom turned the door handle and bumped it open with her hip. "Hey, there, Jet puppy." She set her box on the table and rumpled the old dog's soft ears. "Jet, I could curl up on that blanket with you. What a day! I'm wiped."

Kirsty plunked her box on the kitchen counter. "Mom?"

"Hmm?" Mom had picked up the mail from the table. "Look at all these bills!" She ripped open an envelope and frowned. "How could paint cost so much?"

"Dad said it'd cost a lot to fix up this place."

"Your father has never even seen this house, so how would he know?"

"He was right," Kirsty muttered.

"What did you say?"

"Nothing. Mom? Can I talk to you about something?"

"Of course you can, dear. Go ahead. Hey, get those shoes off right now! You're tracking mud everywhere. Jet, do you need to go outside? Come on, boy."

"Mom!"

"Yes, Kirsty, I'm listening." Mom went into the pantry beside the door. "Pass me that bag of flour, will you?"

"Mom, please! Just stop for a moment."

Her mother came out of the pantry and picked up a carton of milk. "Kirsty, what is it?"

"I want to talk to you about a pony."

Mom put the milk inside the fridge and closed the door with a sigh. "A pony." She raked her hand through her hair, making the spikes stand on end. "You haven't said anything about a pony for a long time now. I'd hoped you'd gotten over wanting one."

Kirsty shook her head.

Mom studied a carton of peach mango yogurt. "Kirsty, I know I said you could have a pony –"

"Promised," Kirsty broke in. "You didn't just *say*, you *promised*."

"Well, the fact is I shouldn't have said or promised anything."

"What do you mean?"

"Sweetheart, sit down." Mom reached across the table for Kirsty's hand. "Listen, I've done some checking and. . . well, to put it plain and simple, we just can't afford a pony."

"But Mom, what if we got a cheap pony? I mean *really* cheap."

Mom squeezed her hand. "Oh, Kirsty, buying the pony is the least expensive part. I've talked with some people –"

"Who?"

"Darwin's friends. They've had horses for years and they filled me in on all the expenses involved in keeping them. Kirsty, do you realize it costs more to put shoes on a horse than it does to buy shoes for you?"

"But not every horse has to wear shoes. A pony

has really tough feet. He won't need shoes. All my books say so."

"Shoes were just an example of the kind of expenses that go along with keeping a horse. The list is endless! Kirsty, I'm sorry, I really am. I know how badly you want a horse and I should never have raised your hopes up."

"A pony. It's a pony that I want. He's smaller than a horse and won't eat so much."

"Pony or horse, it will also need worming and vaccinations and something called teeth floating. Our land is too rocky and too small for pasture, and it isn't fenced. And fencing! You'd be amazed at how many dollars can go into that alone. I won't get into what even a second-hand saddle and bridle cost." Mom pushed back her chair and rose. "There's just no way I can come up with that kind of money."

"Dad?" Kirsty ventured.

Mom wrinkled her nose. "That's not a good idea. I'm sure money must be tight for him and Janice as well, with a toddler in the house. It certainly was when you were a baby."

"Can't we just ask him? He said to call him if I ever need anything."

"I'd hardly call a pony a 'need,' Kirsty. It's not like a winter jacket or something."

"Why can't we just ask? He can always say no."

"Your father has a new life now, Kirsty. We have to stand on our own feet."

"But —"

"But nothing, Kirsty. We can't afford a pony right now and that's it."

Kirsty was silent. Jet whined at the door. Mom let him in.

"Listen, dear, maybe when I get some bills paid off you can have some riding lessons. I know it's not the same as having your own pony, but it would be better than nothing, right?"

"I've already had lots of riding lessons at camp, remember?"

"I know, but that's the best I can do."

Kirsty shrugged.

Mom flattened a box. "I hope you're not going to sulk about this, young lady."

Kirsty shot her mother a dirty look and fled from the kitchen.

She stomped up the stairs to her room and flopped down on her stomach on the bed. Squishing her nose against the glass of the old window, she could see her pony pushing at the wire of the chicken run, trying to reach the grass on the other side. His water bucket was knocked over. She'd have to fill it again.

Her mother had *promised*. How could she just break her word? It wasn't fair.

Lancelot lifted his head, his tiny ears poking through the bushy mane. His bright black eyes were looking right at her. She tapped the glass and he raised his head higher.

He's mine. I have that piece of paper that says he belongs to me.

Mom was wrong, Kirsty knew she was. It couldn't be that expensive to own a pony. The whole valley was filled with horses and ponies. On the bus ride home from school, Kirsty could barely count them all. They couldn't all be owned by rich people, could they?

Kirsty rolled onto her back and frowned at the horse pictures stuck to her ceiling. More pictures – cut from magazines and calendars – plastered her walls and both sides of the door. Not one looked as handsome as her Lancelot.

Look on the good side, she told herself. *This morning you didn't have a pony and now you do.*

Instantly she felt more hopeful. Mom was always saying things happened for a reason.

She bounced off the bed and thudded down the stairs.

"Hey, keep it down!" called Mom from the tiny living room. She was stretched out on the couch, watching the news. "I'll make supper in a while. I just need to unwind."

Kirsty poked her head into the room. "Sure, no problem."

She went into the kitchen and softly picked up the phone. *You're not doing anything wrong,* she told herself as she dialed her father's cell phone. She stretched the telephone cord into the mudroom.

Janice answered. "Oh, Kirsty! Richard, it's Kirsty! How lovely to hear from you." Her dad's wife spoke loudly. In the background Kirsty heard a child squealing and the rumble of a car engine. They were already on the road.

"Hi. Can I talk to my dad?"

"You sure can. Hang on while he pulls off to the side of the road. Here he is."

A moment later Dad took the phone. "Hey, Kirsty Kid. How's my girl?"

"I'm good, Dad." Her father's voice was faint. Kirsty pressed the receiver tightly to her ear.

"Listen, Kidlet, we've got to be quick. My phone's battery is low, forgot to charge it."

"Oh, Dad."

"Oh, Kirsty. So, did you change your mind?"

"Huh?"

"About coming to Calgary with us. We're getting close to the Rockies, but we could turn around and come back to get you."

"No, Dad, that's not why I called." She'd forgotten this was the weekend they were going to Alberta to visit Janice's family.

"Are you sure? Bet you'd have lots of fun. You'd like Janice's parents, and I know your little brother would love to have you along."

Like it would make any difference to a sixteen-month-old baby. "That's okay, Dad. I'll see you on your way back like we planned. Dad? Dad?"

". . . going dead, Kirsty. Can you hear me?"

"I'm losing you, Dad. Can you hear me?"

". . . want to ask?"

The cell phone was dying.

"Dad, phone me from Calgary, okay? Please?" Kirsty listened but there was no reply. She hung up the phone.

How long would it take them to reach Calgary? Hours and hours, too late for her father to phone back tonight. He'd call her in the morning, and Kirsty would tell him about Lancelot and ask for help. Dad always said to just ask if she needed anything.

She made a pot of herbal tea and carried it into the living room.

"Oh, Kirsty, you darling," said Mom drowsily. "I've got to start supper."

"Don't worry about it, Mom. I can heat up that lasagna that's in the fridge."

"Are you sure? I'll make a salad. You need your vegetables."

"I can do that, Mom."

"Don't forget to wash the lettuce thoroughly. And the tomatoes and cucumber. Be careful not to cut yourself with the knife."

"Mom, I know how to make a salad. I'm not a little kid anymore."

"You'll always be my baby." Mom took a sip of tea and closed her eyes.

Her mother did look more tired than usual. *I'll wait*

till morning to tell her about Lancelot, Kirsty decided, *after I've talked to Dad and come up with a plan.*

Lancelot nickered with joy as Kirsty and Jet came around the back of the house.

"Shh!" Kirsty cautioned. "It's really late." She glanced up. No light flickered on in Mom's bedroom.

The pony made whickering sounds deep in his throat. "Hungry again?" She dumped half of the new bag of oatmeal in his bucket. "Got to save the rest for breakfast."

Lancelot barged past her, shoving his head in the bucket. The moonlight shadowed the hollows between his ribs. Pity welled up in Kirsty's throat. He was so thin under his shaggy winter coat.

"Don't worry, you'll never go hungry again." Even as the words left her mouth, the pony flipped over the empty bucket and snuffled the ground for any stray crumbs of oatmeal. He lifted his head and lipped at the plastic bag cradled in Kirsty's arms. "Hey, we've got to save this for your breakfast."

Lancelot nipped at the pocket of her jeans. Kirsty swatted his muzzle away. The pony shook his head, his ears flattened.

"Okay, okay, if you're really still hungry." She poured the rest of the oatmeal into the bucket, careful this time to stand to one side. By the time she'd returned with a fresh bucket of water, he was finished.

He dozed by the gate, slouched on one hip, his lower lip drooping. Kirsty hugged him tightly and pressed her face into his rough mane. "See you in the morning. I don't have to go to school tomorrow because it's spring break. So we're going to have lots of time together."

The pony sighed deeply. Calling softly for Jet, Kirsty fastened the gate of the chicken pen behind her and went inside the house.

3

"Kirsty? Wake up! Okay, Jet, do your thing."

A slobbery warm tongue swiped over Kirsty's cheek. "Yuck!" She dragged the bedcovers over her head.

"Good boy," Mom laughed. "Kirsty, you can come out now."

Kirsty poked out her head. "Why are you waking me up so early? I don't have to go to school. It's spring break."

"It's after eight, lazybones, and we're late. Come on, get going."

"Late for what?"

"You wanted to come to work with me today, remember?"

Kirsty remembered. She'd phoned her mother last week complaining she was bored. Mom had suggested coming into the office during the school break to do some odd jobs, but now there was Lancelot to take care of. "That's okay, Mom. I've got other things to do."

"What kind of things?"

"Oh, nothing much. Maybe I'll go for a walk. Get

some fresh air and exercise." Kirsty tumbled out of bed and scooped a T-shirt off the floor. The room was bright with sunshine. How could she have slept so late with her pony waiting for her outside?

Mom sat down on the bed. "Why don't you call one of your friends from school?"

"They're all busy." Kirsty dug her jeans out from under her bed, wondering if her mother would notice the white and black hairs sprinkled on them.

"Really? Kirsty, I've noticed you haven't been spending much time with children your own age. How are things going at school?"

"Okay."

"Honey, you know how sometimes we're given something to eat that tastes bad to us so we stick it in the back of the fridge. What happens then?"

"I don't know," said Kirsty, bewildered. Sometimes it was hard to follow her mother's mind.

"Well, eventually it goes mouldy and rotten. That's what happens to bad feelings when you try to hide them away inside of you."

"Mom, what are you talking about?"

"Kirsty, you've been through some very difficult life situations in the last few years. You might find it helpful to talk about what's happened with a professional."

"You mean like a counsellor? No thanks, Mom." Kirsty rolled her eyes as she pulled on her socks.

Her mother sighed. "All right, dear. Just remember,

I'm here for you." She squeezed Kirsty's hand.

Kirsty nodded. Okay, it was time. She opened her mouth and closed it again. Her brain had gone completely blank.

"Yes, Kirsty? Was there something you wanted to say?"

"Uh. . . I want to get dressed," she mumbled finally.

Mom bent her head, letting out another deep breath. "Okay, I'll be downstairs."

After the bedroom door closed behind her mother, Kirsty pulled on the rest of her clothes. She rehearsed opening lines in front of the bathroom mirror while she washed her face and dragged a brush through her hair. "Mom, guess what. Something wonderful has happened!"

Or how about: "Mom, you know how you're always saying things happen for a reason?"

"Kirsty!" Mom shouted up the stairs. "I'm leaving."

"Wait a moment!" She ran downstairs.

Mom slipped on her shoes and picked her car keys off the peg beside the phone.

"Anything you want me to do today?" offered Kirsty.

"I left you a list of chores on the table. Maybe you could get started on your homework instead of leaving it until the last moment."

"Sure, good idea."

"Don't spend the whole day watching TV."

"I won't."

"Make sure you phone me. Mrs. Keller's just across the road if you need anything."

Kirsty made a face, knowing Verna Keller would pop in once or twice during the day to check on her. "Mom, I'm nearly thirteen. I don't need a babysitter."

"I'll be home early today, about four." Mom gave her a hug. "Oh, I nearly forgot to tell you. Your father phoned."

"He did? When?"

"About half an hour ago. You were still asleep so he said he'd call back later." Mom glanced at the clock. "Look at the time! Bye-bye, dear. Take care. Oh, and don't forget to walk Jet."

She'd missed Dad's call. Kirsty groaned under her breath, wondering how long it would be before he phoned again. She would have to talk to Mom first then.

Mom's car started. Kirsty ran outside, waving. Her mother rolled down the window. "You're in your socks!"

"Mom, I've got to talk to you."

"Honey, I'm going to be late for work. Why didn't you say something earlier?"

"Well, I. . . " Kirsty broke off, realizing it probably wasn't the best moment to share the news about the latest addition to the family.

"Is it really important we talk right this moment or can it wait?"

Kirsty hesitated. Maybe it would be better to talk to Dad first and get his support.

"Kirsty?"

"Go to work, Mom. It can wait."

"Are you sure, dear?"

"Yeah."

"Okay, I'll be home just after four and we'll discuss what's on your mind then. How does that sound?"

"That'll be okay, Mom. Have a good day at work."

Mom jammed the car into reverse. Carefully, she backed past the house and down the driveway.

Kirsty gave a final wave and turned around. Only a corner of the chicken pen was visible. If her mother had parked the car just a bit farther ahead the night before, she would have been able to see the entire chicken pen, Kirsty realized, and the skinny pinto pony inside.

She went back in the house and wiggled her damp socks into her runners. *Maybe it would have been better if Mom had discovered Lancelot last night.* She could imagine how it would happen. Her mother would drive up to the parking spot, turn off the car, and get out. She'd look up, see the pony, and. . . scream? Then what would she do?

That was the part Kirsty couldn't predict. She created a scene in her head: Mom *oohing* and *ahhing* over Lancelot, upset about his thin frame and vowing to help Kirsty restore him to health and happiness.

Kirsty played the scene over and over in her mind, basking in the warm glow it gave her. She grabbed the bag of carrots from the fridge and went out.

"Lancelot, breakfast is here. I know, I know, it's

about time but —"

She stopped short. The gate tilted against the fence, pushed off its hinges. The chicken pen was empty.

The whole enclosure had been chewed down to bare dirt. Outside the run, hoofprints criss-crossed the damp earth. Her heart skipped a few beats. One set of tracks ran down the side of the driveway.

She followed them out onto the road and let out a groan. Neatly outlined in the sandy shoulder of the road, the hoofprints stretched off into the distance. Kirsty ran along the side of the road, praying she'd find Lancelot just around the corner.

The tracks were farther apart now and slightly scuffed at the toes. Lancelot was trotting, heading for parts unknown. How could she catch up with a trotting pony?

Her chest burned for air. She slowed to catch her breath. The corner was just ahead. She pushed off again, forcing her legs to move faster. She rounded the corner and there he was, standing in a shallow ditch, frantically cropping the thin young grass and budding brush.

"Lancelot! Here boy, come on!"

The pony jerked up his head. A streamer of brush dangled from his mouth. Kirsty hoped the plant wasn't poisonous.

She'd nearly reached him. Panting, she stumbled to a walk and held out her hand. "Whoa, Lancelot, there's a good pony."

He didn't have a halter on. How could she lead him home? She hadn't thought about that. Would he just follow her?

Lancelot watched her approach with interest, expecting her outstretched hand to hold a treat.

"Oh, Lancelot, you had me so scared. Do you know you could have been hit by a car?"

The pony sniffed at her fingers. Kirsty stroked his neck, sending up a small cloud of black and white hairs. She took hold of a hank of mane and tugged. "Come on, boy. Let's go home." She sighed, relieved, as he moved along with her.

Abruptly, Lancelot halted, throwing up his head. His mane slid out of Kirsty's grasp. He whinnied shrilly, nearly bursting her eardrums.

A rider on a bright bay pony came around the corner at a brisk trot. Lancelot squealed again and dashed over to them. The rider reined in the bay. Lancelot arched his neck and touched noses with the other pony.

"Hey, quit that!" scolded the rider as the bay struck out. "Would you catch your pony, please!" Lancelot was prancing behind the bay. "Hurry, before they kick each other."

"I can't," Kirsty said. "I don't have anything to catch him with."

The rider shot a puzzled look from under the brim of her black helmet. She was about Kirsty's age, maybe older, with bright red hair bundled up into her hat.

The plump pony was a russet brown, just a few shades darker than his rider's hair. He tossed his silky black mane.

"How are you going to get him home?"

"I don't know," Kirsty admitted miserably.

The bay pony stamped a hind foot in warning, swishing his heavy tail. "Well, it's not safe to hang around here. Robin might kick or a car will come."

"What can I do?"

"Look, I bet your pony'll follow mine home. Once he's at our farm we can get a halter on him."

"Good idea!"

"Okay, I'm going to trot so he has to keep moving to keep up and can't wander off. Just turn right onto the next road and follow it until you come to Hillcroft Farm. That's our place. See you soon."

The bay pony sprang off at a strong trot. After a moment's hesitation, Lancelot dashed after them. Kirsty tried to keep pace, but they were soon tiny figures in the distance.

She saw them turn onto a gravel road. When she reached the same point, the two ponies were gone, but the side of the road was marked by their hooves. They had veered up a narrow track winding through a tunnel of shaggy cedar trees. Prickly wild rose bushes overhung the split-rail fence. Kirsty jumped across the ditch and gingerly parted the bushes to reveal a carved wooden sign: *Hillcroft Pony Farm*.

She started up the shady track. As if a bell had

rung, ponies suddenly appeared. Through the wooded fields they galloped, rocketing up to the fences, chunks of wet earth flying from their hooves. They slid to dancing halts, pressing up against the rails, tossing silver and copper and ebony manes. Their nostrils flared like tiny trumpets as they snorted at the stranger trudging up the road.

Kirsty spun slowly around, enchanted. Shimmering in the tree-shadowed light, the ponies were something out of a fairy tale. She paused to stroke a charcoal muzzle. The pony shook his heavy silver forelock over his eyes. He whirled about, and at once all the ponies pranced away back into the trees.

Up ahead a dog barked, voices shouted, and a pony squealed. Kirsty ran.

The cedar trees gave way to pastures and farm buildings. A huge red barn towered over the farmyard like a cathedral, its roof arching to the sky. A white board fence enclosed a riding ring cluttered with brightly painted jumps. The road ended at a tiny blue farmhouse with a covered porch.

A brown-and-white terrier burst out of the barn, yapping hysterically. A girl with bushy red hair like a clown's wig came after the dog. "Stubby, shut up! He's in here, Kirsty."

"How do you know my – Hey, you're Faye! You're in my class at school."

Faye nodded.

"I couldn't tell who you were with your helmet on.

I didn't know you had ponies."

"Didn't know *you* had one."

"I just got him." Kirsty stepped into an alley lined with stalls. Faye stood beside the first one. Kirsty peered through the bars at Lancelot, his head buried in a heap of hay. "Oh, you fed him! That's nice of you."

"He's hungry, really hungry. And skinny, too." Kirsty pulled open the stall door. She threw her arms around her pony's fuzzy neck. "Lancelot, don't ever run away again. You really scared me."

"How'd he get loose?" asked Faye.

Kirsty hesitated, reluctant to let Faye know she kept her pony in a chicken run. "Uh, he got the gate open."

"Some ponies can do that. Better make sure you fix it so he doesn't do it again. He could get hurt running loose like that."

"I will."

Faye went into a room across the alley. She came out with a halter and lead rope. "You can borrow this. Let him finish that hay first before you take him home."

"Sure. Thanks a lot. I'll bring it back tomorrow."

"No rush. We've got lots of halters."

Lancelot sighed in contentment. For the first time since Kirsty had entered the stall, he lifted his head, still munching. He puffed warm air on her cheek, then rubbed his bony head on her shoulder, nearly knocking her over.

"Hey, what do you think you're doing?"

"He's itchy," said Faye. "He needs a good brushing to get rid of all that old hair he's shedding. Does he mind being groomed while he's eating?"

"I don't know. Like I said, I just got him. I don't even have any brushes for him yet," Kirsty admitted.

Faye vanished inside the tack room again. When she came out she was carrying an ice cream pail crammed with brushes. She handed it to Kirsty. "Those are some old brushes we don't use anymore. You can keep them."

"Oh, thank you, Faye. Look, Lancelot, now we can get you all prettied up."

"Well, I've got to get back to work."

"Thanks again!" Kirsty called as the other girl left the barn.

Lancelot sniffed the brushes, checking if they were edible. Deciding not, he went back to his hay.

Kirsty studied the bucket, trying to remember which brush to use first. She knew from her summers at riding camp that there was a certain order in which the different bushes were used, but she couldn't re-call just what it was. What did it really matter? Any brushing had to be better than none at all. She chose a long-bristled brush and began sweeping it over the pony's shoulder. Clouds of hair wafted through the air, tickling her face and coating her clothes.

"You know, Lancelot, I've been going to school with Faye since September and I never knew she lived on a pony farm. How come no one ever told me?" The clopping of hooves on the packed dirt of the alley floor brought Lancelot's head up again. Faye led a stocky, mottled brown pony into the next stall and shut the door.

"You sure have a lot of ponies," said Kirsty. "Do you and your brothers and sisters ride them all?"

"There's just my brother, and he doesn't ride anymore." Faye lifted a grooming kit off a shelf.

"How come?"

"He got his driver's licence a couple of years ago. If it doesn't have wheels he's not interested."

"So why do you have so many ponies?"

"Because we train and sell them."

"You and your brother?"

"My grandma and me." Faye went into the stall.

"Are you going to train that pony?"

"Yup."

Lancelot was lipping up the last few scraps of hay. It was time to go. Kirsty buckled the halter on his head.' "Well, thanks again, Faye. I'll see you when I bring back the halter."

"Bye, Kirsty."

She led Lancelot out of the barn. Right away he spotted a patch of green grass by a fence and dragged her over to it. She let him eat, happy to gaze around her at the acres of fenced pastures full of grazing ponies. Did Faye ride her ponies over those jumps in the ring? Did she take them to horse shows in that horse trailer parked beside the barn?

Was it fair that one person should have so many ponies and a barn stuffed with hay and a tack room full of saddles and bridles and a horse trailer and. . .

"You're still here?" Faye led the saddled pony up beside them.

"Oh, Faye, you are so lucky to have all this!"

Faye smiled for the first time. "I know. I really am."

Kirsty watched her lead the brown pony into the ring and mount. Faye sat easy in the saddle, as if she'd been born there. "I wish – oh, come on, Lancelot, we'd better go home."

She tugged at the lead rope to get Lancelot to pick up his head. He came reluctantly, his toes dragging, twisting his neck around to whinny to his new friends.

"Cut that out!" Kirsty scolded as he whirled about her. "Lancelot, behave."

She couldn't blame him for not wanting to leave. What did she have to offer him at home? No food, no shelter, just a crummy chicken pen.

They reached the end of the gravel road. Kirsty checked both ways for traffic. "Okay, let's go. Lancelot? What's wrong?"

The pony's eyes were half closed. He braced his shoulders, stretching his neck out as Kirsty yanked at the lead rope, but not moving a step.

Kirsty leaned on the rope, pulling with all her strength. She might as well have been trying to move a tree. Lancelot would not budge.

She gave up pulling. "So what are we supposed to do? Stand here all day until you decide to move?"

Lancelot dropped his head and dived into the ditch. He rustled in the bushes, searching for anything green to eat. Kirsty plunged in after him. Twigs clawed at her ponytail. Mud seeped into the knees of her jeans when she slipped. She grabbed his halter. "Lancelot, come on!"

The pony yanked his head away.

Kirsty's stomach was growling. "Look, Lancelot, I haven't had breakfast and I'm hungry too. And cold. So please, will you just come home?" She tugged on the rope.

The pony dug in his heels. He looked back at the farm, neighing for the other ponies as if he'd known them all his life. Then he bunted Kirsty's shoulder, nearly knocking her over.

"What? What do you want?" Lancelot pushed her again. An idea popped into Kirsty's head. "I wonder if. . , Lancelot, come on. We're going to see your buddies again."

4

Faye was cantering the brown pony in a circle around a wiry old woman with sandy red hair when Kirsty and Lancelot trotted into the farmyard.

"Get him off his forehand, Faye," bellowed the old woman.

"He's pulling my arms out, Lucy!"

"Push him up from behind. Come on, girl, work at it."

Kirsty stalled in the middle of the yard, uncertain about interrupting the pair in the ring. She wanted to wait quietly until they were done, except that Lancelot was wildly excited to be back among the other ponies again. He tap danced on the spot, his neck arched like a swan's.

The old woman, Lucy, was striding across the sand, pushing up the sleeves of her plaid shirt. "Something I can do for you?"

Faye was still cantering the brown pony in circles. "Hi," said Kirsty. "Um, I was wondering – do you take ponies here?"

Lucy propped her hands on the hips of her blue jeans. Her forehead was crumpled like a discarded paper bag. "Good gracious, I could hang a hat on this creature's hipbones!"

Kirsty shrank under Lucy's glare. "I know he's kind of thin. . ."

Lucy snorted. "I can't give you much for him, not in this condition. He'll need a lot of feeding up. How old is he, anyway?"

"Twelve."

"Lots of years in him yet. Broke good?"

"Huh?"

"Is he good to ride? Or does he have a lot of bad habits that'll have to be trained out of him?"

"I don't know. I haven't ridden him yet."

Lucy rubbed at her face, pulling the wrinkles up and down. "Well, I'd better try him out. Hang on while I get a saddle and bridle."

"Wait! I don't want to sell him. I just got him and I need a place to keep him for a while. Until we get a place fixed up for him at home."

"You want to board him?"

"That's it. I want to board him here. Not for very long, maybe a couple of weeks."

"Board's usually by the month."

"Okay, a month then. How much would that cost?"

Lancelot towed her to a clump of grass by the ring.

Faye reined the brown pony to a walk and rode over. "How come you're back?"

"You know each other?" asked Lucy.

"We go to school together," Kirsty explained. "I'm Kirsty Hagen."

"Lucy March." The old woman gave Kirsty's hand a firm shake. "I didn't realize you were Faye's friend."

Kirsty smiled weakly, wishing she'd at least sat with Faye at lunchtime. The truth was, Faye was as quiet as a mouse at school. Kirsty had never really noticed her much.

"So why'd your folks get you a pony when you don't have anywhere to put him?"

"Well, it all happened kind of suddenly. . ."

"You're new around here, aren't you?"

"We moved to Armstrong last summer. We used to live down at the coast."

"In the city." Lucy sighed. "Well, I guess we can find somewhere to turn out that rack of bones for a month or so. Board's seventy-five dollars a month. That's pasture board, of course, and no grain. Not that ponies need grain, but yours is going to need some feeding up. We'll see how he does on good hay first."

"Seventy-five dollars," Kirsty echoed. She had eighteen dollars and sixty-three cents left in the tin under her bed. How was she going to come up with the rest?

"Tell your parents they're welcome to come and see the place. Just phone first to make sure we're not busy."

"Oh, my dad. . . he's away right now. And my mom works – a lot."

"Hmm. Don't suppose either of them knows much about ponies?"

Kirsty shook her head.

"Figures," Lucy muttered. "People! Kid wants a pony so the parents get one, just like they're buying a bike or skateboard. Except a pony is a living, breathing animal. You remember that, young lady. You can't park this fellow in the garage when you're bored with him."

"I know," said Kirsty humbly. "I'm going to take really good care of him."

"Lucy!" A boy of about eighteen stood on the front steps of the house. "Phone!"

"Be right there," Lucy shouted. "Come to the house, Kirsty, and I'll get you a copy of our boarding agreement. You can put your pony in the barn."

Lancelot was delighted to return to the barn. He snuffled through the shavings for lone strands of hay.

"You behave, okay?" Kirsty told him. She left the barn and jogged across the yard. Over in the ring, the brown pony walked on a long rein while Faye's legs, free of the stirrups, dangled down his sides. Kirsty waved. After a moment, Faye waved back.

Kirsty went up the wood stairs into the covered porch of the little farmhouse. She stepped over kicked-off gumboots, buckets, and a leather halter and knocked softly on the door. Inside, Stubby erupted into frantic yapping. Kirsty waited and knocked again.

Finally, the boy she'd seen earlier yanked open the door. "Don't keep knocking. It drives Stubby nuts."

"Oh, I'm sorry. Is Lucy here?"

"She's still on the phone." The boy walked away, leaving the door open. He glanced over his shoulder. "Come in."

Kirsty stepped inside and closed the door. Lucy sat at an old table heaped with horse magazines and stacks of paper, a phone clamped to her ear.

The boy was at the sink washing dishes. He grinned, shaking his dark red hair off his narrow forehead. "Better sit down. Lucy could be a while."

Kirsty kicked off her runners. "Where should I sit?"

"Anywhere you can find a seat free."

A pile of newspapers, Stubby, and a very large tabby cat filled the remaining chairs around the table. Kirsty spotted a rocking chair. As soon as she lowered herself into it, the tabby cat jumped into her lap.

"Just push him off if you don't want him there," said the boy.

The cat pricked her knees lightly with needle-sharp claws.

"I don't mind," said Kirsty, though the cat was as heavy as a small bag of sand. A bridle hung on the back of the rocking chair. She rubbed her fingers over the butter-soft leather. Where would she find a bridle for her pony?

Tipping forward, she peered into the next room. Framed show ring photos of ponies lined the walls. The top of the television set was crowded with silver trophies.

The door burst open and Faye came in. "Lucy, are

we going to ride that black pony next? Oh, is she still on the phone?" She kicked off her riding boots and lounged against the wall.

"Someone interested in buying a pony," the boy said. "Aren't you going to introduce me to your friend?"

Faye looked puzzled for a moment. She spotted Kirsty. "Oh, this is Kirsty Hagen from school. And this is my brother Riley. . . " She bared her teeth in a wicked grin.

Riley held up a soapy hand. "Don't you dare."

"Riley Heathcliffe Wilton March!" Faye announced.

"No, no, no! You must never say those words!" Riley clutched his head in mock pain. He flexed his fingers, grimacing. "Now you will pay the penalty."

Faye shrieked and dodged past Kirsty to the far side of the table to escape her brother's reach, with Stubby yipping under their feet. Scowling, Lucy grabbed a magazine and swatted both at them and the little terrier. She scribbled a number on a piece of paper and hung up. "Can't you two behave when I'm on the phone?"

"He started it," said Faye, sticking out her tongue at her brother. He ruffled her bushy hair. "Don't, you're messing it up."

"Am I? Sorry, I couldn't tell." Riley jumped away as Faye swatted at him.

Lucy shook her head. She riffled through a pile of papers. Pulling out a sheet, she handed it to Kirsty. "Give this to your parents to look at. One of them needs to sign at the bottom."

Kirsty managed to dislodge the cat and stand up. "Well, thanks for everything. I'd better get home."

"Your pony'll go out with the youngsters. Faye, show her where their field is."

"You mean he can stay?" said Kirsty. She'd been worried about fixing the chicken-pen door so Lancelot couldn't get out again.

"No sense taking him home to get loose again. Just be sure to get that boarding agreement signed and back to me right away."

"But I haven't got any money with me to pay you."

"Bring it tomorrow with the boarding agreement. Hang on, it's nearly the end of the month. Look, give me twenty-five dollars to cover the rest of this month and then you can pay the full amount on the first of next month. That way my bookkeeping system won't get messed up."

Riley snickered. "Since when did you start a book-keeping *system*?"

"Don't get smart with me, young man," retorted Lucy. "I've been running things this way for a lot of years now." She stuck out her hand. "Welcome to Hillcroft Farm, Kirsty."

Kirsty grasped the knobby fingers and shook. "Thank you. Thank you very, very much."

The phone was ringing as she got in the door. "Hello!"

"Hi there, Kirsty. I finally caught up with you."

"Dad! Oh, I'm so happy you called. I've got to talk to you."

"Well, I'm listening. Fire away."

Kirsty took a deep breath. "Okay. Dad, it's about a pony."

"Oh boy."

"What do you mean?"

Dad sighed. "Your mother warned me the subject of a pony might come up."

"Oh."

"Sweetheart, all girls your age are horse crazy. It's a phase you're going through."

"It is not!"

"Kirsty, owning an animal is a big responsibility. It has to be fed and cleaned and exercised every single day."

"Dad, I *know* all that."

"Just remember the goldfish."

Kirsty squirmed, reliving the horror of finding three little bodies floating in their aquarium. She'd been so sick with guilt when she realized she'd forgotten to feed them for four days that she couldn't eat her supper. "Dad, I was only eight years old. I'm nearly thirteen now."

"That's another thing. This fall you'll be in high school. You're going to have a lot more homework to keep up with. Janice told me how much time her pony took up when she was your age, and frankly,

Kirsty, I don't see how you can fit one into your schedule."

"You won't even let me try. That's not fair!"

"Kirsty, we're talking a very expensive animal here – both to buy and look after."

"But Dad, I've found a really great place to board him, and they only charge seventy-five dollars a month. If you could pay that –"

"Did your mother put you up to this?"

"No, she didn't! She doesn't know anything about this."

"Hmm."

"So will you? Pay the seventy-five dollars a month?"

There was a long silence. "Kirsty, this isn't something we can decide over the phone. We'll talk about it when we come back from Calgary."

"But Dad, I've found a pony for only a hundred dollars! I just need a place to keep him."

"We'll discuss this when we get to Armstrong, okay?"

"Okay," she agreed glumly.

Dad wouldn't arrive until the next week. That still left ten days until the next month's board was due. Right now all she had to do was come up with the twenty-five dollars she owed Lucy for the rest of March. There was eighteen dollars and sixty-three cents upstairs in her tin. She needed six dollars and thirty-seven cents more.

That wasn't that much money. She'd get it some-how. And, she recalled, growing cheerful again, Dad hadn't said no.

"Kirsty! The house looks wonderful!"

"Hi, Mom! Want a cup of tea?" Kirsty waved to the tea tray on the kitchen table. The boarding agreement was beside the tray, under a permission slip for a school field trip that also needed to be signed by her mother. A pen sat on top of the papers.

"This is so thoughtful of you." Mom shrugged off her coat and hung it on a peg by the door. She rubbed Jet's ears and sniffed. "You smell nice, old man."

"I gave him a bath," said Kirsty. "I did all the chores on the list *and* I washed the windows."

"You washed the windows? All of them? No wonder it's so bright in here."

"Yeah, well, they were pretty dirty."

"My goodness, Kirsty, I can't believe you did so much work." Mom sank into a chair and poured a cup of tea.

"Mom?" Kirsty sat across from her.

"Yes, dear. What do you want?"

How did she always know? "I was wondering — could you pay me for washing the windows?"

Mom smiled, reaching for her purse. "All right. You did do a lot of extra work. How about five dollars?"

"Okay. And can I have my allowance early? I'm saving up for something," she explained.

Mom handed her a ten-dollar bill.

"Thanks." Kirsty slumped in her chair, relieved. "So did you have a good day?"

Mom waggled a hand. "Let's just say it was a challenging day."

"What does that mean?"

"Well, for one thing, the volunteer who was organizing the bottle drive this Saturday left for Ontario a few days ago because of a family emergency and forgot to tell us. So guess who's in charge of putting the bottle drive together."

"You?"

"That's right. Darwin, too. Oh well, it's just a bottle drive. How hard can it be? So, dear, what did you want to talk about?"

Kirsty took a deep breath. "Well, I was at a friend's place today. She lives on a pony farm with her grandma and brother."

"Do I know this friend?"

Kirsty shook her head. "Her name's Faye March. She's in my class at school, but we've never hung out together."

"So how did you end up at her farm today?"

"Oh, I was outside and Faye came riding along. We started talking and then went over to her place." Every detail was true; she'd just left a few bits out.

"Kirsty, you know you're supposed to phone me and tell me when you go somewhere. I need to know where you are."

"Sorry, Mom," Kirsty said meekly.

"Just remember next time, please. So you've got a friend with a pony."

"Not just one pony – a whole farm full. Her grandma buys them for Faye to train and then they sell them."

Mom sipped her tea. "I wonder why she and her brother live with their grandmother. Where are the parents?"

"I don't know."

"A pony farm, huh? Does her grandmother teach riding lessons? Maybe you could have some if they aren't too expensive."

Kirsty brightened. "I'll ask. But I know how much Mrs. March charges for boarding a pony. Only seventy-five dollars a month! Pretty cheap, right?"

Mom grinned, shaking her head. "Kirsty, you just don't give up, do you, dear?"

"But, Mom –"

Someone knocked on the back door and Jet scrambled up, barking.

"That'll be Darwin," said Mom. "Come in!"

"What's Darwin doing here?" asked Kirsty.

"Oh, didn't I tell you? We've got to do a lot of phoning about the bottle drive tonight, so Darwin offered to bring Chinese food. Here, let me take that." Mom got up as her co-worker came through the door, his arms full of brown paper bags.

"Hi there, Kirsty," said Darwin. "How's it going?"

"Okay," she replied. Any other time she'd have been happy to see him. "What's happening with your hair?"

"You like it?" Darwin bent his head for her to admire his black buzz cut.

Kirsty made a face. "I kinda liked your hair a little bit longer."

"Me too," the young man admitted. "But hey, you gotta try something different once in a while, right?"

"I guess so."

Darwin set the bags on the table. "Let me clear that stuff out of the way," said Mom, picking up the papers and the pen. "Wait a second, Dar. I'll just sign these and Kirsty can put them away."

She scanned the field trip form and scribbled her signature on it. The boarding agreement had slid out from underneath. "This too?" Mom wrote her name and handed both papers to Kirsty. "Run these up to your room and put them somewhere safe. We don't want to be hunting for them when you go back to school."

"Sure, Mom." Kirsty hesitated.

"Hurry now, the food's getting cold."

Kirsty rushed upstairs clutching both forms. Her heart was thumping wildly as she slipped the boarding agreement into her sock drawer. She pressed her fist against her chest, trying to slow it down.

She hadn't done anything wrong, she told herself sternly. It was silly to feel guilty. She would tell Mom about the boarding agreement later, after Darwin left, if it wasn't too late and Mom wasn't tired and cranky. Or maybe she'd get up early tomorrow and take Mom a cup of coffee in bed. That might be a good time to talk.

Kirsty dragged open her eyelids. She swatted at her clock radio, trying to stop the buzzing of the alarm. At last she succeeded in switching it off. She snuggled back into the cozy warmth of her bed.

Downstairs, a cupboard door slammed. Kirsty sniffed. Coffee? Oh no, Mom was up already. She scrambled out of bed and scurried down the staircase.

Mom sat at the kitchen table with a cup of coffee and the phone pressed to her ear. She frowned and tapped a pen on a tablet of paper. "Yes, I know you're busy, Gail. We all are. But it's only a few hours of your time. Yes, of course I understand. Bye." She hung up.

"Mom! How come you're up so early?"

"Good morning to you too, dear." Mom held out her arms for a hug. "We need more drivers for the bottle drive. I'm trying to catch people before they go out."

Kirsty hugged her mother. "How's it going?"

"Not very well," sighed Mom. "It's always the same people who volunteer." Shaking her head, she sipped her coffee.

Kirsty stepped back, judging her mother's mood. Mom crossed a name off the list on her tablet with a quick slash of her pen. Clearly, she was annoyed.

Kirsty decided to hold off telling her about the boarding agreement. Mom obviously had enough on her plate right now. This evening, after she got home from work and had eaten supper, would be a much better time.

5

"Kick him, Faye," shouted Lucy. "Come on, *make* him canter!"

Faye smacked her heels against the grey pony's sides. The pony swished his tail and trotted faster around the ring.

Kirsty leaned against the fence a few feet away from Lucy. The old woman squinted into the morning sun, her gaze fixed on the girl and the pony.

Faye kicked again. The grey pony dropped his head and sprang up into the air.

"Hang on!" called Lucy.

Faye's black helmet bobbed wildly. Kirsty could see daylight between her and the saddle. "She's going to fall off!"

Lucy ducked through the fence. Faye wrapped her hands in the mane and somehow managed to kick the pony again. Suddenly he shot forward at a canter, his charcoal-black legs churning through the sand. "Look out!"

Her grandmother scurried out of their path. A grin creased her face. "Good girl," she said softly, squeezing back onto the other side of the fence.

After a few rounds of the ring, Faye pulled the grey

pony up and patted his damp neck. She was smiling, her cheeks bright pink. "I'll try him again after he's caught his breath." This time when she asked him, the pony arched his back in a half-hearted crow hop before lurching into a canter.

"A couple more times, then put him away," said Lucy. She turned to Kirsty. "Morning."

"Good morning."

"Hope your pony's better behaved than that." Lucy jerked her head at the grey pony.

Kirsty nodded, hoping so too. She dug in her pocket. "I've got the board money. And here's that form." She held out a fistful of bills and coins.

Lucy arched her sandy eyebrows. "A cheque would've been okay. I kinda expected to see your folks." She unfolded the form and studied it carefully.

"My mom had to work. But she'll come over soon. Maybe tonight."

"We won't be home tonight."

"Oh. Well, maybe tomorrow night."

Lucy folded the boarding agreement and slipped it into the back pocket of her jeans. "Your pony's in the corral by the barn. There's not a lot of grass yet in the fields, but we're introducing him to it slowly."

"So he doesn't colic, right?"

"That's right. You know about colic, eh? That's good."

"I went to horse camp for four summers. They taught us lots of stuff. And I read a lot."

"Reading's good. Just remember you can't learn it all from the books. Okay Faye, that'll do. You can cool him out now." Lucy walked off toward the pastures.

Kirsty headed to the barn. She whistled. From around back, Lancelot whinnied.

"Hi there, fella! How are you?"

The pony nickered, pressing up against the tall rail fence. Kirsty climbed over and dropped down inside the small enclosure. Lancelot nuzzled her fingers and lipped at her pockets. Finding them empty, he returned to the pile of hay in the corner.

"Is eating all you think about?" teased Kirsty. She leaned on his shoulder as he ate, inhaling his grassy scent. His strong teeth munched steadily on the dried stems. She ran her hand along his thin neck, picturing it curved and thick like Faye's ponies.

Her hand came away matted with hair. She went into the barn and got the brushes Faye had given her.

Ages later, Lancelot's fuzzy coat was a bit less shaggy. Most of the dreadlocks had been combed out of his mane. The white patches were certainly brighter and the black patches gleamed. Kirsty's arms and back burned from brushing non-stop. Lancelot was still eating.

His head swung up. Faye was at the corral gate with a wheelbarrow and stable fork. "I've got to pick his corral."

Sighing wearily, she set the wheelbarrow in the gateway and began forking up the manure. She was still dressed in riding clothes – jodhpurs, ankle boots, and fleece jacket – but she'd pulled off her gloves and helmet. Her red corkscrew curls were gelled with sweat.

"Can I do that too?" asked Kirsty as Faye flipped a forkload of manure into the wheelbarrow.

"Sure, but you don't have to. It's part of your board."

"I want to help. It'll be fun."

Faye's pale eyebrows twitched, just like her grandmother's. "Okay. There's another fork in the barn, hanging on the wall."

"So how many ponies do you have?" asked Kirsty. She stabbed her fork into a heap of dark green droppings and heaved the manure into the wheelbarrow. It was heavier than she'd expected and she managed to leave half the pile behind.

"Around twelve. One of them might be sold, though."

"Are you going to miss him?"

"Yeah, but he's going to a good home."

"Do you ride them all?"

"Pretty much. Lucy rides a few, and some of them are just babies yet. I'd have a lot more time to ride if I didn't have to go to school."

"But everyone has to go to school!"

"Why?"

"Well. . . because you've got to learn things. So you

can get a job when you're grown up."

"I'm going to be a professional rider. School's a waste of time for me. Come on, we're done here."

They trundled the wheelbarrow to the manure pile behind the barn and dumped it. Faye set her fork on her shoulder and pushed the wheelbarrow into the barn at a trot. "Did you bring your tack?"

"No." Kirsty placed her fork in a hanger on the wall. "I, uh, don't have any yet."

"Are you going to ride him with a halter?"

"Ride him?"

"Yeah. He is broke to ride, isn't he?"

"Oh, for sure. Mr. Jensen's grandkids used to ride him."

"So let's go for a ride." Faye went into the tack room. "You can borrow this hard hat. And here's a bridle you can use. Does he go in a snaffle?"

"I guess so." Kirsty stepped inside. Bridles and saddles hung in tiers on one entire wall.

Faye looked at Kirsty's feet. "You're wearing boots. Good. So now we just need to find you a saddle and girth. Go get Lancelot and put him in a stall so we can see what saddle fits him."

A short time later Lancelot was outfitted in a polished brown saddle with a matching bridle. The round silver rings of the snaffle bit were so shiny Kirsty could see her reflection in them.

"Tuck your hair up inside the helmet," Faye advised. "Lucy hates messy hair. Okay, you're ready.

Why don't you warm up Lancelot in the ring while I get Robin tacked up?"

Kirsty led Lancelot by the reins to the riding ring. She was about to ride her own pony for the first time. Her head felt light. She was grateful for the sturdy black helmet weighing it down.

The stirrup iron clanged on the gate as Kirsty led Lancelot through. Alarmed by the sudden noise, the pony sprang forward, yanking on her arm. "Whoa!"

Lancelot stopped, head high and eyes bulging. He snorted, stamping his foot. Kirsty's stomach quivered.

I can't do this! As soon as the thought crept into her head, she squashed it flat. This was her pony, Lancelot. She had to ride him.

She fastened the gate securely. Lancelot seemed to be calming down. He dropped his head, snuffling at the sand in case something edible appeared.

"Come on, Lancelot, let's go for a walk around the ring." She led the pony slowly around. "We always did this at riding camp before we got on."

After two circuits, Kirsty stopped the pony in the centre of the ring. It was time. She lifted the reins over Lancelot's head and pulled the stirrup irons down the leathers. Grasping the left stirrup iron with her hand, she struggled to lift her foot high enough to reach the stirrup. She hopped up and down on her other foot and finally slid the toe of her boot onto the tread. Grabbing a hank of mane, she pushed off with her right foot. Suddenly the stirrup dropped down and the saddle slipped over Lancelot's shoulder. Kirsty kicked her foot free and jumped back to solid ground.

She'd forgotten to tighten the girth. How many times had the instructor at riding camp reminded her to make sure the girth was snug before getting on? Hot-faced, she pushed the saddle back into place. She lifted the saddle flap and buckled the girth two holes tighter.

"Okay, let's try again." She stabbed her toe into the stirrup, bounced twice, and swung aboard.

She was on. She froze in the saddle, her hands clutching the reins, startled by the abrupt change of view. From up here, Lancelot's black ears were longer and in the middle of her line of vision. His mane was a broad wedge of hair. The ground was far away and the fence circling the ring seemed much lower.

Lancelot surged forward. Kirsty swayed with the motion. He shook his head, fighting her death grip on the reins and yanking Kirsty's arms down. She tipped to the front of the saddle.

The pony broke into a trot, jouncing her so hard her teeth banged together. Her feet fell out of the stirrups. She snatched at his mane to hang on.

"Lancelot, whoa!" she moaned. She tipped to one side, hanging over the pony's shoulder.

Abruptly, Lancelot stopped, throwing his head high. Kirsty wriggled back into the saddle.

Faye led Robin out of the barn and into the ring. "How's your pony going?" She tugged down her irons and swung lightly into the saddle. Robin champed softly on his bit, waiting patiently until Faye gave him the signal to walk.

Lancelot dashed alongside the bay pony. "He's a bit frisky," Kirsty said.

"So's Robin in the spring." Faye studied Kirsty jiggling in the saddle as Lancelot pranced beside her pony. "You should ask your mom if you can have lessons from Lucy."

Kirsty's heart leaped at the idea. She could see herself riding like Faye, back straight and arms still, while Lancelot strode quietly beneath her, his neck curved, gently chewing his bit.

"She probably wouldn't charge you very much," Faye went on, "since you're already boarding your pony."

Money again. "I'll have to ask," Kirsty said, knowing she couldn't.

Faye nudged Robin into a sedate trot. Lancelot bounded after them. By hanging onto the reins as hard as she could, Kirsty was able to keep him from running into the other pony's hind end. She tried to copy Faye's posting, rising up and sitting down in time with the one-two beat of the trot.

"Let go of his mouth," Faye said, glancing back. "You're balancing on the reins."

Kirsty slipped Lancelot a few inches of rein and snatched it back when he shot ahead.

And then she was doing it, rising in time with her

pony, up and down, up and down. It was as easy as riding a bicycle. Lancelot let out a long snort, obviously relieved she wasn't thumping on his back anymore. He flowed beneath her, more powerful than anything she'd ever felt before. With Lancelot she could run faster, fly higher, travel farther than she'd ever be able to by herself. He was more than a pet or friend; he was her partner. No matter what problems lay ahead, she knew she'd done the only thing she could have done.

"Did you have a nice time at your friend's today?" asked Mom that evening.

"It was great!" said Kirsty. "She lives on this neat farm with this huge old barn and lots and lots of ponies."

"Sounds like your idea of heaven."

"Oh, Mom, it's. . . " Kirsty closed her eyes, picturing herself trotting on Lancelot in the white-fenced ring while Faye popped Robin over the brightly coloured jumps. "It's just wonderful."

"Well, it must be a pretty special place since you didn't make it home until nearly suppertime." Mom shoved the spade into the damp earth. They were at the back of the house, trying to dig up a small patch of nearly flat ground to plant a vegetable garden. Mom stomped her foot down on the edge of the spade. It barely budged. Mom waggled the handle, only managing to lever out a small heap of soil. She stretched, rolling her shoulders. "This is killing me."

Kirsty jabbed at the ground with her spade and flicked up a small chunk of sod. "Face it, Mom. This isn't going to work."

"I'm not giving up yet. If one way doesn't work, there's got to be another. Somehow, I'm going to have a garden."

"Nothing is impossible, right, Mom?"

"Absolutely right, Kirsty. Where there's a will, there's a way. Listen, I really want to come over and meet Faye and her grandmother."

"They want to meet you too, Mom."

"Okay, then. As soon as this bottle drive's over with, we'll go visit Hillcroft Farm. Sound good?"

"Sounds good, Mom," agreed Kirsty, relieved. Dad would be back from Calgary and she'd have everything arranged by then.

6

"Oh, Kirsty, I'm glad you're here!"

"What's the matter, Faye?" Kirsty crouched down and gently shook Stubby's paw.

"Some people are coming by to try out Happy, and he's filthy. Lucy and Riley have gone to Armstrong to get parts for the tractor and I'm way behind on the chores."

Kirsty held up her hand. "I'll do the rest of the chores while you clean up Happy. What time are these people going to be here?"

"I forgot to ask."

"So they could arrive any time. We'd better get moving."

Kirsty had watered all the ponies, picked out the corrals, and cleaned Happy's tack by the time Lucy's old red pickup careered up the driveway and screeched to a halt at the house. Brushing Lancelot at the hitching rail outside the barn, she could hear Lucy scolding Riley as she eased out of the passenger seat.

"Crazy kid," she grumbled, stomping over to the barn. "Drives like a maniac. Morning, Kirsty." She scooped up Stubby and rumpled his ears.

"Hi, Lucy."

Lucy's sharp green eyes ran over Lancelot. "He's put on a few pounds already. Not a bad-looking pony."

Kirsty beamed. This was high praise coming from Lucy.

"Lucy!" Faye burst out of the barn. Her hair had sprung out of her ponytail and she was covered with light brown pony hair. "Some people called Waddell are coming to try out Happy."

"They were supposed to be here tomorrow." Lucy frowned, putting Stubby down. "Okay, let's get him cleaned up."

"All done. I even trimmed his fetlocks and washed his tail."

"Good girl. Now, what chores still have to be done?"

"None. Kirsty did them all."

A smile spread slowly across Lucy's face. "Well, what a team you two make. I'm proud of you both."

Kirsty's face was suddenly warm. She bent her head, picking the hairs out of her dandy brush with her fingers.

"Well then, ladies, let's head to the house for an early lunch before anyone arrives," said Lucy.

Just a few minutes after noon, Stubby bounded to his feet and threw himself at the door, yipping hysterically.

"Looks like our company's here," remarked Lucy. She slipped on her boots and went out to greet the visitors.

"Hey, there's another car coming," said Faye.

Kirsty followed her down the porch stairs. A small, dark blue car bumped up the driveway. It continued past the barn to the house. Kirsty caught her breath. The blue car parked and her mother got out.

"Hi, are you Lucy March?"

"Yes, I am." Lucy strode across the yard, hand outstretched.

Mom returned the handshake. "Linda Hagen. I'm Kirsty's mother."

"I'm very pleased to meet you, Linda." Lucy glanced back at Kirsty, huddled behind Faye at the foot of the stairs. "Your daughter's a fine girl. She's been a real help to us around the farm this week, let me tell you."

Mom spotted Kirsty and waggled her fingers in a wave. "She seems to be over here all the time. I hope she's not wearing out her welcome."

"Not a bit. My granddaughter Faye really enjoys the company." Lucy turned around. "Girls, would you head over to the barn and tell the Waddells I'll be right with them?"

"Sure, Lucy. Come on, Kirsty." Faye tugged at Kirsty's sleeve. "Kirsty?"

"Huh?"

"Come on." She towed Kirsty along.

"Aren't you even going to say hi?" asked Mom.

"Oh, hi, Mom," she said as they jogged past.

"What's wrong?" asked Faye. "You're acting weird."

Kirsty stopped in her tracks. Faye swung around to face her. "She doesn't know I have a pony," Kirsty blurted out.

Faye blinked. "*Who* doesn't?"

"My mother. I got Lancelot without telling her."

Faye's mouth made an O that grew bigger and bigger.

"I know I have to tell her," Kirsty went on, "but what if she says I can't keep him? I can't give up my pony, Faye. You understand, don't you?"

The other girl nodded slowly.

"Faye," called Lucy, "get a move on!"

Still speechless, Faye resumed walking to the barn. Kirsty started after her.

"Kirsty! Come here, please," said Mom.

Through the open barn doors she could see Lancelot's head hanging over the stall door. He was watching her, his black eyes bright under his fuzzy forelock. For a moment, Kirsty imagined leaping on his back and galloping away into the mountains.

A hand settled on her shoulder. She whirled around.

"Can't you hear your mother calling you?" said Lucy. "Are you feeling sick, girl? You're as pale as a ghost."

Kirsty shook her head.

"Well then, go talk to your mom. She's got something to tell you." Lucy gave her a little push.

Mom was leaning against the hood of her car with

her arms crossed. She tipped her head back to face the sun.

The blood thumped in Kirsty's head like a drumbeat. Fists clenched, she walked toward her mother.

7

"Kirsty, get a move on. I have to get back to work."

The toes of Mom's sandals came into view. Kirsty halted. She looked up. Mom was frowning, her mouth stretched in a thin line.

"Are you all right? You don't look very good. You're not coming down with the flu, are you?" She pressed her wrist to Kirsty's forehead. "Do you feel like you have a fever?"

Kirsty shook her head.

"I just finished talking to Mrs. March," said Mom. "We didn't have any time to go into details, but. . . "

She paused. Kirsty watched her mother's grinning face in dismay. Was she actually *enjoying* this?

"She's agreed to give you riding lessons! Well, what do you think? Isn't that great?"

Kirsty couldn't seem to make sense of what she'd just heard. "Riding lessons?" she echoed.

Mom nodded. "I know you had your heart set on your own pony, but lessons will be fun, won't they? Kirsty, what is the matter? I thought you'd be thrilled."

"I am," said Kirsty. "I'm just so. . . surprised. Are you sure you can afford riding lessons?"

"Don't you worry about that, dear," said Mom, waving away her concern. "There is one more thing. Mrs. March said it would be better for you to ride one of her well-schooled ponies at first rather than Lancelot. Apparently this Lancelot pony is rather 'green' when it comes to ringwork, whatever that means. Does that make any sense to you?"

"Uh-huh." It was startling to hear her mother say Lancelot's name. Why wasn't she upset?

"Is Lancelot a pony you've become fond of?"

"Yeah." So Lucy hadn't given her away. Here was her chance to explain about Lancelot. Kirsty opened and closed her mouth like a fish gasping for air. Her brain was completely empty of words.

Mom glanced at her watch. "Oh, wow, look at the time. I've got to run, sweetheart. I've got an appointment at one back at the office." She held out her arms.

Kirsty hugged her mother. "Thanks, Mom."

"You're welcome, dear. I know how much riding means to you. I just wish I could afford to get you a pony of your own."

"Well, what'd she say?" hissed Faye after Mom's little car had bounced down the driveway.

She sat next to Kirsty on the fake stone wall jump. A small, stocky boy wandered slowly around the ring on Happy. His parents watched proudly, chattering to Lucy without taking their eyes off their child.

"I'm getting riding lessons," said Kirsty. "Here, with Lucy."

"That's great! What about your pony? What did your mother say about Lancelot?"

"She still doesn't know."

"Kirsty!"

"Faye, I didn't have a chance to tell her. She had to get back to work right away."

"You've got to tell her."

"I've been trying, but she just won't listen."

"What do you mean?"

"Every time I start to talk about a pony, my mom just jumps right in and says we can't afford one. She won't even talk about a pony with me."

"That's not fair!" said Faye.

"My mom *promised* me I could have a pony when we moved here. Then someone told her how expensive it is to keep a pony and she changed her mind."

Faye gasped. "She just broke her promise to you?"

Kirsty nodded. "So I'm trying to look after Lancelot by myself for a couple of days until my dad gets here. I know he'll pay the board."

"Wait a moment. Your mom signed the boarding agreement. How could she do that without knowing about Lancelot?"

Kirsty plucked at the white hairs on her jeans. "Uh, she just signed it along with another form from school."

"You mean she doesn't even know she signed it?" Faye's eyes were round. "Kirsty, that's illegal or something. We've got to tell Lucy!"

"It's just for a few more days. Once I talk to Dad, I'll tell my mom. She'll have to let me keep Lancelot if Dad's paying the board."

"I don't have a good feeling about this," said Faye miserably.

"Me neither," Kirsty admitted, "but what else can I do?"

"Can't you tell your mother and *she* can ask your dad to pay the board?"

Kirsty snorted. "You don't know how stubborn my mother is. She's got this thing about making it on her own, and she refuses to ask Dad for any help. And if I ask him she gets mad at me. But this time I don't care."

"I don't like lying to Lucy," said Faye.

"It's not really lying," protested Kirsty. "Just pretend you don't know anything about it."

Faye pulled a strand of hair straight. She let go and it sprang back into a spiral. "But I do, don't I? I know all about it."

"Kirsty!" Riley knelt beside the carcass of the tractor. Scattered on the ground were greasy bits and pieces of the machine. He waved an arm, beckoning. "Got a message for you."

Faye and Kirsty walked across the yard toward him. "Is Riley really going to be able to get that tractor running?" asked Kirsty.

"He sure will. Riley can do anything mechanical."

Riley looked up as they came close. He swiped at his face with the back of his oily hand, leaving a black smear on his chin. "Your mom phoned. She's got a meeting in town tonight so she's going to pick you up right after work and take you out to supper."

"Then what? She's not going to make me go to that meeting with her, is she?"

"Think so. She said something about not wanting you to be all by yourself in the house until late."

Kirsty groaned. "That's going to be so boring!"

"You could spend the night here," said Lucy, coming up behind them in time to overhear the conversation. "We'd be glad to have you."

"Yeah! That's a great idea," said Faye. "We could sleep in the hayloft."

"I'll call your mother if you want to stay."

"Yes, please!" said Kirsty fervently.

8

Something damp and cold rooted at Kirsty's neck. With a squeak of alarm she sat up in her sleeping bag. Stubby's beady eyes stared at her intently.

"Go away," she muttered, snuggling back down into the sleeping bag. Stubby poked his cold nose into her neck and whined. She nudged Faye's shoulder. "Wake up. Your dog has to go."

Snoring, Faye flung out an arm. Kirsty ducked just in time.

Stubby whined again. "Okay, okay, I'm coming." The little terrier quivered as Kirsty wiggled out of the sleeping bag into the chilly air. She pulled on her jacket over the flannel pyjamas Faye had lent her, tucked Stubby under one arm, and went backwards down the ladder from the hayloft to the barn floor below. Stubby squirmed free as she stepped off the ladder and scampered out the open door. Kirsty followed him outside.

The ponies grazed peacefully in the grey early morning light. Lancelot lifted his head and nickered as Kirsty ran over to him in bare feet. She climbed up on the bottom rail of the fence and threw her arms around his fuzzy neck. He put up with her hug for half a minute before pulling free and returning to eating.

Kirsty pressed her hand against his ribs. They were already padding out with extra flesh. She felt reassured. Whatever else she had done wrong, she'd done the right thing for Lancelot.

"He's put on some weight already," said Faye, coming up silently in bare feet. Her sleeping bag was draped over her shoulders like a shawl.

"I think so."

Faye rubbed at her eyes with the heels of her hands. "Why are you up so early?"

"Stubby woke me up."

Both girls turned to glare at the terrier snuffling the fence posts. "Bad dog," scolded Faye. Stubby wagged his tail and kept on sniffing.

Faye yawned. "I'm still sleepy."

"I thought horse people got up early," said Kirsty.

"On horse show mornings I do." Faye paused. "When I was little we used to go for breakfast rides. We'd pack our saddlebags full of food and go up the mountain to a special spot and have breakfast there."

"We?"

"Lucy and me and Riley. Before he found wheels."

"Oh, Faye, let's do it."

"Go on a breakfast ride? But you've never been on a trail ride."

"Yes I have. I went on lots at riding camp. And Mr.

Jensen said Lancelot was really good on the trails."

"I don't know, Kirsty. Maybe we should wait until later."

"I can't go riding later. My mom's making me help with her bottle drive, remember? If I'm going to ride I've got to do it now."

"Maybe we should stay in the ring."

Kirsty rolled her eyes. "I'm tired of just going round and round in the ring. C'mon, Faye, let's go for a trail ride. What's the big deal, anyway?"

"Okay, but we've got to be back in time to do chores."

For such a skinny pony, Lancelot had a surprising amount of energy. He marched briskly up the trail at the back of the farm, forcing Robin to trot to keep up.

"Slow him down," called Faye from behind.

"I can't," said Kirsty. She tightened the reins and Lancelot tossed his head, fighting the pressure of the bit on his mouth.

The trail widened and Faye urged Robin up beside them. "I think we should go back."

"Why?"

"Lancelot isn't fit enough for such hard work."

"But he's got lots of energy! He wants to go."

The trail entered a stand of trees, forcing Faye and Robin to fall back. The track angled sharply up a steep slope. Kirsty grabbed handfuls of mane to keep from sliding down her pony's rump. With relief, she realized his pace was slowing.

They burst out of the trees into a meadow. "Stop here!" shouted Faye. Kirsty untangled her hands and pulled Lancelot to a halt. He dropped his head, his sides heaving. Kirsty slid down, her legs trembling. The pony's neck and chest were damp with sweat. She braced herself as he rubbed his itchy head on her shoulder.

"Don't let him do that," said Faye. "It's a bad habit." She jumped off Robin. The bay pony was hardly puffing. "You'd better walk Lancelot around until he cools down."

Both ponies wore their halters under their bridles. Faye slipped Robin's bridle off and tied him to a sturdy tree. She loosened his girth and unbuckled the canvas saddlebags bulging with food they'd raided from the kitchen. She spread the bounty on a stone outcrop at the edge of the clearing – muffins, cheese, apples, bananas, and tiny cartons of juice.

"We used to build a fire and make coffee for Lucy and hot chocolate for Riley and me." Faye gestured to a metal cylinder just over half a metre high. "That was our firepit. Hey, don't tie Lancelot so close to Robin. They might kick each other."

After tying her pony on the other side of the clearing from Robin, Kirsty grabbed a muffin and a banana and sat down on a rocky ledge. The sun's rays angled through the trees, warming their faces. The ponies slouched their hips and dozed.

"We should do this every single morning," said Kirsty, peeling the banana.

Chewing a mouthful of apple, Faye grunted in reply.

When she'd eaten all she could, Kirsty lay on her back on the ledge, the sun covering her like a blanket.

"We have to go back soon," said Faye drowsily.

"Uh-huh." Kirsty shifted position. The rock ledge was becoming bumpier. Her fingertips brushed through a tiny crevice and traced a shallow straight line. Other lines branched off it. Some lines curved; some were straight.

Kirsty sat up and looked down at her hand. "Look, Faye, someone's carved their initials in this rock. RM. Oh, and GM. I wonder who they are." She twisted around. "Here's more. LM, FM, and LM again. The trail here runs right from your farm. Do you think it's anyone you know?"

"Riley March. Glen March. Lisa March, Faye March, and Lucy March." Faye folded her legs and rested her chin on top of her knees. "My brother, my parents, me, and my grandma."

"Your parents?" Kirsty frowned. "But where are they?" As soon as the words fell out of her mouth she knew she'd said something wrong.

Faye could have been carved out of the rock she sat on.

"I'm sorry," said Kirsty softly. "I didn't mean. . . "

"They're dead. They died in a car accident when I was six." Faye's voice was flat.

Kirsty dithered, fearful of saying the wrong thing again. Eventually, too much time passed and there was nothing to say.

"We should head back," said Faye finally. She gathered up the remnants of their feast and stuffed them in the saddlebags.

"Faye, I'm sorry," Kirsty said again as they mounted the ponies.

Faye nodded. "Come on, let's go."

Lancelot jigged down the trail, refreshed by the rest and eager to get home. If Kirsty reined him in, he shook his head and pranced sideways, tripping over rocks and rotting logs. She glanced back at Faye for help. The other girl was off in a world of her own, her expression blank. Robin dawdled underneath her, scuffing his toes and snatching mouthfuls of brush. Lancelot bounced around a bend in the trail and Faye and Robin were out of sight.

Kirsty's legs were aching and her insides so shaken up she doubted they'd ever fall back into the right places. Lancelot missed a dip in the trail and stumbled, snapping her neck. She gasped at the sharp pain and jerked the reins, even though she knew it was just about the worst riding sin she could commit. Every joint and muscle in her body was crying out in pain. She wondered if she should get off and walk home. Would her legs still work?

Lancelot slid to an abrupt stop. He threw his head up and blasted through his nostrils like an old-fashioned steam engine. Brush crackled and a large brown deer bounded away through the trees.

The pony whirled about, his neck and shoulders ducking out from under Kirsty. Her feet flew up in front of her. She grabbed for mane to hang onto and came up with handfuls of air. Her shoulders slid down Lancelot's neck. Then she was hanging over his shoulder and tumbling to the ground. Panicked, she threw out her arms to break her fall.

She hit the ground and rolled onto her back, spitting out dirt. Pain shot along her right arm in throbbing waves. She sat up, hunched over her injured arm, moaning in agony. Her stomach heaved and she thought she might throw up.

"Kirsty! What happened?" Faye jumped down from Robin and slung her arm through his reins. She knelt beside Kirsty. "Are you hurt?"

"Don't touch me!" shrieked Kirsty. She hugged her injured arm across her body.

"Kirsty, where does it hurt?"

"All over. My arm." The pain was settling down, except in her wrist. She looked and saw it was already swollen. "I think it's broken!"

"I'll ride home and get help."

"Don't go!"

"But Kirsty —"

"Don't leave me alone," she begged. She didn't want

to be left out here in the bush all by herself. "Please, Faye."

"But what am I supposed to do? You need help."

Taking a deep breath, Kirsty shifted onto her knees. "Help me get up."

"You shouldn't move," protested Faye. "That's what I read in a first aid manual."

"I'm okay." Her stomach had quietened down. She held out her good arm, and Faye pulled her to her feet. "Maybe a little dizzy." Using Faye as a support she hobbled over to a tree and leaned against it.

"How are you feeling?" Faye watched Kirsty anxiously.

"Okay, I guess. Stiff and bruised." She flexed her wrist slightly and whimpered at the pain. "My wrist hurts."

Faye unclipped Robin's lead shank from his halter. "We'll use this as a sling. Put your hand on your shoulder."

"Do you know what you're doing?" asked Kirsty as Faye strapped her arm close to her body with the thick cotton rope.

"Riley took a first aid course and he would practise on me. There, how does that feel?"

Kirsty tested her arm. It nested snugly in a coil of rope. "That helps."

Faye nodded with satisfaction. "All right. Now we have to get you home."

"Where's Lancelot?" Kirsty looked around.

"He must have gone home after you fell off. What happened, anyway?"

"A deer scared him. He turned around so quickly I couldn't stay on."

Faye grimaced. "Lucy's going to kill me."

"Why? What did you do wrong?"

"I should never have taken you out of the ring. You're just a beginner and Lancelot's a lot of pony for you to manage."

"I'm not a beginner rider," Kirsty said. She caught Faye's sideways look. "Well, I guess compared to you I am. Don't worry, I'll explain to Lucy going for a trail ride was my idea."

"I'm still going to be in big trouble," Faye predicted gloomily.

Behind them, branches snapped. Kirsty stiffened. "What was that?"

Lancelot emerged from the trees, twigs skewered in his bushy mane. He snuffled Kirsty's cheek and sighed.

"Oh, Lancelot, you came back."

Faye snagged his dangling reins and ran her hands over his legs. "He looks okay. But he's broken the buckle on the reins."

"I'll pay to have it fixed," said Kirsty.

Faye tied a knot in the leather reins. "It's a long way back to the farm. Do you think you could ride Robin if I ride Lancelot?"

"But I want to ride Lancelot."

"Kirsty, don't be stupid! Do you want to fall off again? We're already in a whole lot of trouble."

"Is Lucy really going to be angry?" asked Kirsty quietly.

Faye snorted. "She's going to go nuts. I'll be lucky if she takes me to a single horse show this season."

"But it's not your fault I fell off! That deer scared Lancelot."

"Of course it's my fault. I'm the experienced rider. I should have known better than to take a greenhorn and a badly trained pony out on a trail ride. We didn't even tell anyone where we were going or what time we'd be back. I've broken every rule there is, Kirsty, and I'm in deep trouble. So will you just get on Robin without arguing!"

Meekly, Kirsty allowed herself to be boosted onto the bay pony. She gritted her teeth when her injured wrist pressed against his withers. It was strange to see Robin's broad russet neck rising up in front of her instead of Lancelot's fuzzy patchwork.

"He neck reins, so you can hold both reins in one hand," Faye said. She led Lancelot up to a stump and swung her leg over him. "I'll go in the lead. Just let Robin follow. Okay?"

Kirsty nodded. Robin stepped carefully beneath her, as if he knew she was hurt. She sighed. The steady swaying motion was a lot more comfortable than Lancelot's bone-rattling jigging.

Her wrist began to throb again in the rope sling.

She suddenly felt worn out and very weak. It seemed like her head was drifting up above the rest of her body.

Lancelot was striding out with Faye. No throwing his head about or prancing sideways down the trail. Dimly, Kirsty wondered what Faye was doing to make the pony behave so nicely.

They'd been travelling downhill through the trees forever. Just when Kirsty had begun to despair of ever finding their way out of the forest, the trees gave way to the rolling green pastures of the farm.

The ponies picked up the pace. "Whoa!" Kirsty moaned as Robin broke into a trot. Amazingly, he did, flicking an ear at her voice and returning to his steady walk.

They crossed the grass field and passed through the gate. The ponies' hooves clopped loudly on the hard-packed dirt of the farmyard.

Short of the barn door, Faye reined in Lancelot. Robin stopped beside them. "Oh boy," breathed Faye.

Lucy was framed in the barn door, her hands on the hips of her jeans. A fierce scowl creased her face.

"Where in the blue blazes have you two been?" she thundered. Her frown vanished. "Kirsty, are you okay?"

Robin swayed underneath Kirsty. Lucy and Faye seemed far away at the other end of a shrinking black tunnel. Then the darkness covered everything.

Lucy grabbed Kirsty as she fainted.

9

Kirsty's mother pushed through the crowd in the hospital emergency room to reach the reception desk.

"My daughter! She's been hurt! Where can I find her?" she demanded shrilly.

"Please calm down, ma'am," said the hospital clerk. She tapped at the keys of her computer. "What's your daughter's name?"

"Kirsty Hagen. She was brought in a couple of hours ago."

Through the babble of voices in the emergency room, Kirsty heard her name. She stood up. "Mom? I'm over here."

Her mother spun around. Barging past a nurse and an elderly man, leaping over the footrest of a wheelchair, she reached Kirsty and grabbed her shoulders. "You're okay! Thank goodness." She flung her arms around Kirsty. Her name tag from the bottle drive dug into Kirsty's cheek.

"Easy, Mom," Kirsty wheezed. "I need to breathe."

Mom released her and stepped back. Her eyes widened. "What's that? What have you done to your arm?"

Kirsty held up the splint. "It's just a bad sprain, Mom. I didn't break it, but it really hurts."

Mom pushed her fingers through her hair, making it stand up in spikes. "How did you hurt your arm?"

"I, uh, fell off."

"What do you mean? Fell off what?"

Lucy pushed herself up out of the plastic chair. She motioned Faye to stay seated. "She came off her pony. He spooked and she lost her balance. Nothing to get too wound up about."

"She fell off a pony?" Mom echoed. She shook her head. "How could that happen?"

"You've got to understand, Linda, that falling off is part of riding. There's an old saying: seven falls make a rider."

"But I didn't know you were already giving her riding lessons! Don't you need my permission on a piece of paper or something? Really, Lucy, I don't think this is very responsible of you."

"Now, who said anything about riding lessons? Kirsty and Faye were out trail riding on their own ponies."

"What are you talking about? Kirsty doesn't have a pony."

Kirsty sank into a chair beside Faye.

"Sure she does." Lucy eyed Mom uneasily. "He's been at the farm all week. You signed the boarding agreement."

"Lucy, I wouldn't have signed a boarding agreement

because we don't have a pony," Mom said, speaking very slowly.

"I'm not losing my mind," retorted Lucy. "There's a pinto pony eating down the grass in my pasture, and your daughter says he belongs to her. I've got a piece of paper in my desk, signed by you, stating that you agree to pay me seventy-five dollars a month to board this animal. What's going on here?"

Crossing her arms, Mom turned to the girls. "That's exactly what I'd like to know. Kirsty, *what* is this all about?"

Kirsty shrank into her chair. She'd never seen her mother look so angry. "It's a long story, Mom."

"I don't care how long it is! You tell me what you've been up to. I want every last detail, do you understand?" Mom tapped her foot on the vinyl floor. "Come on, start talking."

"I, uh, got a pony."

"You did *what?* Without telling your own mother?" Mom's voice rose.

"I meant to, but. . . " Kirsty broke off, knowing she didn't have a good reason to offer.

People were watching them. A nurse came over. "Is there a problem here?"

Mom took a deep breath to compose herself. She managed to smile politely at the nurse. "We're fine, thank you."

The nurse gave her a sharp look. "There are some forms to be signed at the desk."

"I'll be right there." Mom leaned close to Kirsty. "We'll continue this discussion in the car." She turned away and spoke to Lucy before going back to the desk. Lucy sat down again, rubbing her creased forehead.

Kirsty banged her head against the hard plastic back of her chair.

"Your mom's really upset, huh?" said Faye softly.

"Yeah. You were right; I should've told her a long time ago."

"Uh-huh. Now what's going to happen?"

Kirsty huddled deeper in her chair and shook her head. She'd never done anything like this before in her entire life. She couldn't imagine how Mom would punish her. "It doesn't matter what it is," she whispered to herself. "As long as I've got Lancelot I can go through anything."

"Maybe Lucy could try and calm her down," suggested Faye.

"I don't think *anybody* could calm Mom down right now," said Kirsty gloomily.

Her mother dropped the pen on the desk, swung around, and beckoned to Kirsty. Reluctantly, Kirsty stood up. She looked down into Faye's worried face.

"See you," she said.

"Yeah," said Faye. "See you too."

"Kirsty, I'm waiting," Mom said sharply.

"Bye, Lucy." Kirsty willed the old woman to look up at her. Lucy's eyes remained fixed on the floor.

Her heart heavy, Kirsty left Faye and Lucy and followed her mother out of the hospital.

Mom slammed the car door shut so hard the whole car rattled, startling an elderly couple walking through the hospital parking lot. "How could you do this, Kirsty? How could you be so sneaky and underhanded?"

"I'm sorry, Mom," said Kirsty miserably.

"You know what hurts the most? That my own daughter would lie to me! Look me in the face and lie to me." She pounded her fist against the steering wheel. The spikes of her hair quivered, like tiny porcupine quills.

"I didn't mean –"

"Didn't mean'? I don't care what you meant or didn't mean to do. You lied to me, Kirsty! You deceived me! Why? Why did you do it?"

Kirsty hung her head. "I'm sorry."

"Is that all you have to say? That you're sorry?"

"I tried to tell you, but you wouldn't listen."

"Oh, so that made it all right for you to go ahead and get this pony."

"He only cost a hundred dollars. It was my own money."

"And then you signed my name to a legal document! That's forgery, young lady, do you know that?"

"No it wasn't. I gave you some forms and you just

signed them all without looking at them."

Mom pinched the bridge of her nose. "I can't believe this! Where did I go wrong with you?"

"I'm really sorry, Mom. I won't ever do anything like this again. I promise."

"You promise?" Mom snorted. "How can I believe in your promises, Kirsty? How can I trust you anymore?"

Switching on the ignition, Mom shoved the car into gear and drove out of the hospital parking lot. Kirsty pressed her nose against the glass of the passenger window. She'd really messed things up. She should have told Mom about Lancelot as soon as she'd got him. Mom would have been upset, but not as angry as she was now after finding out her daughter had kept the pony a secret from her. How long would it take her to calm down?

She peeked across the car. Thin blue veins stuck out of Mom's clenched hands. She drove with her chin thrust forward, her mouth pressed into a tight line.

Kirsty's heart sank.

A shiny silver car was in the driveway when they arrived home.

"Great," muttered Mom.

"Dad!" Kirsty fumbled for the door handle with her good hand. She scrambled out of the car and threw herself into her father's arms. "You weren't supposed to be here until Monday!"

"Kirsty Kid!" He swung her around. "We came back early to spend more time with you. Hey, what's this? What have you done to your arm?"

"Oh, Kirsty," cried Janice, "have you broken your arm?" She came up beside them, a wriggling toddler and a toy truck in her arms.

Kirsty held up the fibreglass splint. "I sprained my wrist. No big deal."

"How did you do that?" asked Dad.

"I, uh, fell off a pony."

"A pony! No one told us you were taking riding lessons." Eyebrows raised, Dad looked at Janice.

Before Kirsty could explain, Mom was there. "She's not taking riding lessons, Richard."

"I used to fall off my friend's pony all the time," said Janice. "We would ride double bareback, and when that pony got trotting we'd bounce around so much we'd slide right down her side."

"I don't think you understand the whole situation, Janice," sniffed Mom. "The pony Kirsty fell off apparently belongs to her!"

"When did you get Kirsty a pony?" said Dad.

"That's the point, Richard! I didn't. She went out and bought this pony without my consent!"

"How much did you pay for it?" asked Janice, setting Brandon down and handing him the toy truck.

"A hundred dollars," said Kirsty. "It was my own money."

"What a steal!" Janice
ing after Brandon as
clutching the truck.

"How could you not
pony?" Dad asked Mom.

"Because she went to
from me! She even tricked
to a boarding agreement."

"Just the same, you mus
thing." Dad rubbed his chi
time does Kirsty spend on h   you're at
work?"

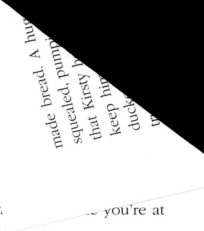

"Are you saying I neglect my daughter?" Mom's
voice was dangerously quiet.

"Well, Linda, you've got to admit there is something wrong when a mother doesn't know her own
daughter has acquired a large animal like a pony.
Overlooking a hamster or a guinea pig I could understand, but a pony?"

Kirsty slunk away to the house and let Jet out. She
huddled on the veranda steps trying not to hear her
parents bickering, while the old dog snuffled about
on the lawn.

"There you are." Janice settled down beside her.
"Here, hold onto your brother, will you?" She plunked
the toddler and truck in Kirsty's lap.

A pair of wide hazel eyes stared up at her. He was
surprisingly heavy, like the big bag of flour Mom
bought when she was in the mood to make home-

_e_ grin split his round face. He
_ng_ his sturdy arms and legs so hard
_d_ to hold tight with her good arm to
_from wiggling right out of her grip. She
_d_ to avoid being hit in the head by his plastic
uck.

"Oh, you like big sister, don't you, Brandon?" cooed
Janice. The toddler chuckled and smacked his truck
on Kirsty's splint.

"Can you take him back, please?" Kirsty asked. "He's
hurting my arm."

Janice swung the baby onto her own lap. "How
does your arm feel?"

"It still aches, but it's a lot better than before. I can
move my fingers now."

"That's good. So it's back to school on Monday."
Janice bent down to pick up the truck Brandon had
tossed to the ground.

"Yeah." Kirsty fell silent. School seemed like another life right now.

Jet woofed. "Who are you barking at, you silly dog?"
said Dad, walking across the lawn. He rumpled the
Labrador's soft ears. Jet leaned against Dad's knees,
wuffling happily. "I miss you too, old fellow."

"Richard, I was thinking," said Janice. "Maybe we
could go see Kirsty's pony?"

Dad nodded. "Where is he, Kirsty?"

"I keep him at a friend's farm. It's not far away."

"Excuse me!" said Mom, overhearing. "Kirsty is not

to go anywhere near that animal!"

"But, Mom!"

"No, Kirsty. The pony will be sold and that's final. I've already spoken to Lucy March about getting rid of it."

"No!" screamed Kirsty. "He's mine. I bought him with my own money."

"And then you lied to me and deceived me!"

"Calm down, Linda," urged Dad. "I'm sure we can work this out."

"There's nothing to work out. The pony has to go!"

Kirsty ran into the house and slammed the door. The old walls shook. Mom's favourite picture crashed to the floor, shattering the glass.

Good, thought Kirsty fiercely, *good*.

10

Rain rattling on the metal roof of the old house woke her. Kirsty pushed back the bedcovers and sat up. Jet was stretched out on the bed beside her, snoring. Mom must have let him in last night, after she'd cried herself to sleep.

She got up, threw on some clothes, and went across the hall to use the bathroom. Downstairs in the kitchen, voices murmured, Dad's among them.

Kirsty peeked through the door. Mom and Dad sat at the table. Janice crouched on a blanket on the floor with Brandon, who was spinning the wheels of his toy truck with his chubby fingers. Mom stared sourly into her coffee cup. Dad leaned across the table. He said something and Mom shook her head.

"That's not all. She tricked me into signing my name on a boarding agreement!" Mom said.

"Didn't you pay attention to what you were signing?" asked Dad.

"I *thought* I was signing a permission slip for a field trip. Anyway, there's no way I can afford to support a pony."

"Perhaps we could help out," suggested Janice.

"Absolutely not," said Mom.

"Oh, come on, Linda," said Dad. "Don't be so pig-headed."

"Richard, our daughter has to learn a lesson. She cannot deliberately keep the truth from me and expect to be rewarded for it."

"I'm sure Kirsty didn't do those things on purpose, Linda," said Janice. "Maybe she finds you hard to talk to."

"I work very hard at keeping the lines of communication open with Kirsty. There's nothing she can't talk to me about."

Brandon spotted Kirsty and screeched happily. She stepped into the room.

"Well, look who's finally awake!" said Dad. "Good morning, sleepyhead."

"Morning," mumbled Kirsty. No way was she going to call it good.

Brandon trundled up to her, his arms held wide.

"He wants you to hug him," explained Janice.

Hesitantly, Kirsty crouched down and put her arms around the baby's sturdy body. Brandon bumped his truck against her shoulder and squealed with delight. Kirsty patted his silky, pale blond head.

"Good morning, dear," said Mom.

Kirsty ignored her. She looked at Janice. "Hi."

Someone banged on the door. Jet lumbered down the stairs, barking.

"Who on earth?" Mom was saying when the door

flew open and Faye burst in. Her hair sprang wildly from her head in a mass of wet red curls.

"Lancelot's gone! I can't find him anywhere!" Faye wrapped her arms around herself, trembling.

"What do you mean?" demanded Kirsty, scrambling to her feet. Brandon howled, startled by the loud voices.

"He got out of his corral. I guess I didn't shut the gate properly. Riley and I have looked all over the place for him."

Mom brought Faye a towel. "Here, dear, dry your hair and face and sit down. I'll make you a cup of hot chocolate to warm you up."

"But we've got to keep looking," said Faye, as Janice helped her remove her soaking wet jacket.

"A few minutes won't make much difference," Mom told Faye. She plugged in the kettle. "Now, does your grandmother know you're here?"

Faye shook her head. "Lucy left early to trailer Happy to his new owners. She won't be back until this afternoon. Riley's at home phoning all the neighbours to ask if they've seen a loose pony." Faye turned to Kirsty. "We've got to find him before something happens to him. He could get hit by a car or fall into a ditch –"

Kirsty jammed her feet into her shoes. "Come on, we've got to keep looking!"

"We'll all search for the pony," said Janice, scooping up Brandon. "If we split up we can cover a lot of ground."

"Any idea what direction he took, Faye?" asked Dad.

"No, the rain washed away his tracks."

"Wait a moment!" said Mom.

Gathered at the door, the others looked back at her.

"Kirsty suffered a serious injury yesterday. Have you all forgotten that?"

"Mom, I'm fine," insisted Kirsty. "Please don't make a big fuss about nothing, not right now."

"Kirsty, that's enough," Dad ordered.

She gaped at him. "But —"

"Your mother's concerned about you. We all are. You gave us quite a scare. Don't worry, Linda, we'll make sure she doesn't overdo it."

"Thank you, Richard, but I can take Kirsty and Faye in my car."

"You're going to help us look for Lancelot?" said Kirsty in disbelief.

"Of course I am. We can't just leave the pony wandering loose. Come on, let's get going."

Mom stuck her head out the window as Faye and Kirsty walked back to the car. "Anything?"

"No," said Kirsty glumly. "They were inside all morning because of the rain."

"I can't believe all the people in all the houses we've stopped at didn't see a black and white pony running loose," said Faye. She pulled open the car door and slid inside. "He didn't just disappear into thin air."

"We're due to meet up with the others in fifteen minutes," said Mom. "We'll have to start back."

"Can't we go just a little bit farther?" begged Kirsty. Her wrist was aching again, but she made herself ignore it.

"We're almost in town. I don't know much about ponies, but surely he'd head the other way, where there are open fields and grass, instead of toward houses and cars."

"I don't understand why he left the farm at all," said Faye. "Our ponies don't get out very often, but when they do they hang around eating grass and teasing their buddies. We've never had one leave home before."

"He must have wandered off and lost his way back," said Mom, turning the car around.

"No." Faye shook her bushy head. "A pony has an excellent sense of direction. He always knows his way home."

Home? The word echoed in Kirsty's head. She caught her breath. "That's where he's gone! I know where he is!"

"It's the next house," Kirsty directed from the back seat, "the one with the For Sale sign on the fence."

Mom parked next to the weathered grey house. "It

looks like no one lives here."

Kirsty jumped out of the car and ran through the wet, shaggy grass to the back of the house. Rusted farm machinery hunkered in the weeds. A door sagged open on a tumbledown shed behind them. She forced her way through snags of weeds and old tires and peered into the shed. Her heart sank. No pony.

"Kirsty? Where are you?" called Mom.

"Over here by the shed." She broke off, listening. Something scraped against the outside wall of the shed.

Kirsty pushed through a budding lilac bush on the other side of the shed.

Lancelot whickered softly. Kirsty's heart leapt and tears of relief filled her eyes.

She wrapped her arms around his neck and rubbed her face in his bushy mane. His neck was soggy and cold against her skin. "Oh, Lancelot, we've been looking for you everywhere."

The pony started as the others came around the side of the shed.

"Oh, thank goodness, you've found him!" said Mom, picking her way through the knee-high weeds.

"Is he all right?" asked Faye.

"I think so," said Kirsty. "He's really wet. He must have been standing here for hours."

Faye felt the tip of the pony's ear. "He's cold. We've got to get him warmed up." She took a handful of mane just behind the ears and tugged. "C'mon,

Lancelot, get moving."

Lancelot jerked away.

Kirsty stepped back to help. The hem of her jeans snagged in the weeds. She yanked her leg, but the heavy fabric was still caught. She crouched down to pull it free and froze.

Snaking through the weeds, barbed wire twisted and coiled around Lancelot's legs. The tiny spikes had razored his skin, criss-crossing his limbs with skinny, red stripes of blood.

"Oh no!" Kirsty tugged frantically at the wire. As she pulled, the barbs hooked together and tangled even more. They bit into her hands, stinging.

"Don't do that." Mom grabbed her arm, pulling it away. "We need some sort of wire cutter. I'll go look in that shed."

Lancelot shifted, lifting one front leg.

"Steady now, there's a good boy," breathed Faye. "Careful Kirsty. If we startle him, he might panic."

Feeling the pressure of the wire, Lancelot bobbed his knee twice. He threw up his head, flattening his ears.

"Whoa, Lancelot, take it easy," crooned Kirsty. To her relief the pony lowered his leg. He shuddered and let out a long sigh.

Helplessly, she stroked his neck over and over, murmuring encouragement. Lancelot's head sagged. His busy radar ears were still and his black eyes gazed dully into space. "Hang on, Lancelot. We're going to get you out of this."

Mom appeared. Her hands were empty. "I can't find anything to cut that wire."

Panic rose in Kirsty's throat, choking her. "What are we going to do?"

"Kirsty, stay calm. We're not beaten yet. I'll drive home and check our tools."

"We've got wire cutters at the farm," said Faye. "Riley knows where they're kept."

"Okay, I'll go to the house and phone him."

"Please hurry!" urged Kirsty. "I don't know how much more Lancelot can take."

Mom squeezed her shoulder. "I'm on my way."

Lancelot was shivering. "He needs a blanket or something to keep him warm," said Kirsty.

"I'll look around and see if I can find anything," said Faye.

"It's going to be all right," Kirsty chanted over and over. Lancelot barely responded to the sound of her voice. He was breathing so quickly, like a dog panting after a long run. A coil of barbed wire scratched at his belly with every breath.

Cautiously, Kirsty shuffled around to the pony's side. She raised her leg and pressed her foot down on the wire. The strand curved downwards. Kirsty lowered her leg, pushing the strand of wire all the way to the ground. She slowly lifted her foot, feeling the wire spring back and then catch on another coil of wire.

She took her foot away. Two strands of wire were now hooked together by their barbs. She trod up and down the length of the coil, flattening the wire.

"What are you doing?" Faye had returned, packing a bundle of old burlap sacks.

"Bring those here. Lay them on top of that wire, there, where it's flat."

"Good idea, Kirsty!" Faye stepped on the piece of wire beside Kirsty, crushing it flat. Side by side they shuffled along the snarls, slowly pressing the wire flat.

Kirsty gasped as a coil lashed out from the tangle, ripping through the knee of her jeans.

"Are you okay?" asked Faye.

"Yeah." The skin of her knee burned from the cut. Kirsty forced herself to ignore the pain. It was only a scratch compared to what Lancelot was enduring.

Their progress was slow. The steps had to be close together to squash the wire flat. Too far apart and it snapped back up, sharp barbs raking like wild animal claws.

"Give me a rag," said Kirsty. She wrapped the old sack around her hands and reached out to push down the wire that was between Lancelot's legs.

Sensing freedom, the pony jerked his legs. "Whoa, Lancelot, stand still now." Kirsty hunkered down, pushing the wire low enough for Faye to stamp on it. Lancelot's knee brushed her ear.

"Kirsty, get back!"

Kirsty reached up and laid her hand on the pony's leg. "You've got to stand still, Lancelot, so we can help you."

She felt the pony's muzzle brush the top of her head. "That's right, it's me down here. Okay, Faye, hurry."

Kirsty stayed at Lancelot's head until all the wire was flattened. Faye helped her lay all the burlap sacks on the wire. "Come on, Lancelot, you can move now. That's a boy."

The pony took a cautious step. Feeling no restraining wire biting into his legs, he crouched down and bounded forward. He stumbled a few steps and halted, his nostrils wrinkled with pain. Kirsty's insides twisted sharply. Her pony's legs were swollen to the size of fence posts, with blood seeping from a myriad of gaping cuts.

Faye swore softly. "Lousy barbed wire! Why do people just leave it lying around? Don't they know what it does to animals?"

The lilac bush rustled. "Lucy, they're over here!" shouted Riley. "You got him out!" He stopped short at the sight of Lancelot, back hunched and tail clamped tight. "Oh no."

The others emerged from the lilacs. Lucy was last. She scowled fiercely. "What a mess."

"You can fix him, can't you, Lucy?" asked Kirsty.

"Oh, Kirsty, I don't know." Lucy rubbed her wrinkled cheeks. "We brought the horse trailer. Riley already called the vet. He's going to meet us at the farm."

"But Lancelot's going to be all right, isn't he?"

"Of course he is, sweetheart," said Dad, but Lucy shook her head.

"He's cut up pretty bad, Kirsty. But we'll wait until the vet's examined him before we do too much worrying. Come on, let's get this fellow home to the farm."

Riley returned with a halter and lead rope. He had to bend over to buckle the halter on Lancelot's sagging head. "Let's go, boy."

Lancelot stiffened against the tug of the halter. Lucy slapped him on the rump.

"Don't hurt him," cried Kirsty.

Lucy shot her a look as the pony hobbled past the lilac bush. "Sometimes, Kirsty, you've got to do what's best for the animal, even if it hurts a little. You remember that."

11

The veterinarian arrived at the farm just as they were unloading Lancelot from the horse trailer. He pulled up the pony's lip to examine his mouth. "His gums are pretty pale. Get him into a stall quickly, folks."

Dr. Kelly listened to Lancelot's heart with his stethoscope. He stepped back, hanging the instrument around his neck. "How long has he been like this?"

"Couple of hours at least," said Lucy, throwing a quilted blanket over the pony.

The vet nodded grimly. "Let's get an IV started. He needs fluids. Faye, give me a hand."

Kirsty winced as the vet deftly inserted a needle into Lancelot's neck. The pony didn't stir. Dr. Kelly attached a length of thin tubing to the needle. The other end of the tubing ran into a clear plastic bag full of a colourless liquid. The vet turned the bag upside down and passed it to Faye. The liquid ran down the tubing, through the needle, and into Lancelot's vein.

"Okay, fellow, let's have a look at these cuts." Dr. Kelly crouched down, examining the pony's legs and chest carefully. "Hmm, you've made a mess of yourself. Lucy, I didn't think you had any barbed wire on this place."

"I don't, Keith. This pony got loose and decided to head back to his old home. That's where he did this."

"Whew!" The vet straightened up. "I wish there was some kind of law against people leaving barbed wire lying around. Well, Lucy, which way do you want to go with this one?"

"That bad, eh?"

"I'm afraid so. You know yourself how hard it is to treat lower leg wounds. Every time the pony takes a step he'll pull them open again."

"The thing is, Keith, it's not my decision to make. The pony belongs to young Kirsty here."

The vet regarded Kirsty gravely over the top of his glasses.

"You can make him better, can't you?" asked Kirsty.

"You're the parents?" Dr. Kelly looked past Kirsty. "You should know the situation is very serious."

"Just how bad is he?" asked Mom.

"Bad. He's in shock and the injuries are severe. Even if the lacerations heal up, there will most likely be scar tissue that could inhibit his usefulness."

"So what do we do?" asked Janice.

"There are two options. First off, there's not much I can do in the way of treatment except suture some of those lacerations, give him a tetanus shot, and start him on antibiotics. He's going to need complete stall rest for a couple of weeks. The wounds will need ointment applied several times a day. He'll need antibiotics every six hours."

"Sounds like a lot of work," said Dad.

"It is," agreed the vet. "You could send him to my clinic, where he'd get round-the-clock nursing care, but of course that would be very expensive. And really, there's nothing we would do at the clinic that you couldn't do yourselves, provided you have the time to devote to the animal's recovery."

"And what's the other option?"

The vet pushed his glasses back up over his nose. "Euthanasia."

"You mean put him to sleep?" cried Mom.

Dr. Kelly nodded.

Kirsty reeled in horror. From far away she heard Lucy's voice, felt her strong hands guiding her onto a hay bale and lowering her head to her knees. "Take a deep breath. That's it. Nice and slow."

Gradually the barn stopped spinning around her. Mom sat down on the bale and stroked her hair gently.

"I know it's a lot to take in, folks," said the vet, "but we need to put those sutures in soon. That is, if you decide to go ahead with the treatment."

"Go ahead and stitch him up," said Mom.

"It's all my fault. I should have double-checked the gate." Faye plucked a stem of straw off her jeans and tied it into a knot.

"It's not your fault, it's mine," said Kirsty. They were seated on a hay bale parked in the open door of Lancelot's stall, with Stubby in between them. The pinto pony stood with his eyes half closed in the corner, the same spot he'd been in all evening. He hadn't even sniffed the bucketful of young grass Kirsty had gathered. "I thought I could take care of a pony by myself, even though everyone told me I couldn't. . . and they were right."

"You did your best," Faye said.

Kirsty shook her head. "My best wasn't good enough. Lancelot deserved better. I just hope that he goes to a good home."

Stubby shot off the bale and trotted to the barn door. He tipped his head, whining.

Mom came in. "Hi, girls."

"Mom! What are you doing here? Riley was supposed to drive me home."

"I wanted to see how the pony's doing." Mom peered in the stall.

"About the same," said Kirsty.

Mom bit her lips together. "He looks so sad. He must really hurt."

"He does. Mom, would you like to meet him?"

"Oh, I don't want to bother him."

"Please, Mom. He's really nice."

Faye tugged the bale away from the door. "Come on in, Mrs. Hagen."

Mom stepped into the stall. "Hello, Lancelot. Pleased to meet you."

"Pet him," urged Kirsty. "Like this." She ran her flat hand down the pony's neck.

Gingerly Mom brushed her hand over the pony. "Good boy, Lancelot. That's a good pony."

The pony's ear twitched. He bent his neck around and nuzzled Mom's jacket pocket. Finding it empty, he dropped his head and lipped up a mouthful of hay.

"He's eating again!" said Faye. "That's a good sign."

"How's our patient?" asked Lucy, poking her head in the door. "Looking a lot brighter. And eating too."

"He just started," said Kirsty.

Lancelot hobbled forward and doused his muzzle in the water bucket. He gulped noisily until the bucket was nearly empty.

"He's on the mend," said Lucy. "Now, Linda, there's something I've got to talk to you about. You've made it clear how you feel about Kirsty getting this pony –"

"I don't appreciate being lied to by my own daughter," Mom said stiffly.

"I'm with you there," Lucy agreed. "That's not something I'm going to forget in a hurry." She fixed a look at Kirsty, who blushed and busied herself straightening Lancelot's blanket over his back.

"I'm not going to change my mind about selling the pony, if that's what you want to talk to me about," said Mom. "Even if I could overlook the fact she deceived me, she's much too young to be responsible for such a large animal. This whole situation proves that."

Kirsty pressed her face against Lancelot's neck, trying to hold in her tears.

"I agree that Kirsty is pretty young to be caring for the pony all by herself," said Lucy. "But that's not what I want to talk to you about. This pony's got to heal before anything can be done with him. Looking after him's going to take a lot of time, and it's already hard to find enough hours in the day to get our work done."

"Oh. Well, do you have any suggestions about where else we could take him?"

"Hang on a moment. There's no need for you to take the pony away. I'm going to need extra help around the farm, and it makes sense to me that Kirsty should give up some of her free time after school to lend a hand with the chores."

"Oh, please," Kirsty began.

"But Kirsty has a sprained wrist," Mom cut in.

"Even one-handed, there are a lot of things she could help out with around here," Lucy went on. "Cleaning tack, scrubbing buckets, stuff like that."

"She'd have to keep up with her school work," Mom cautioned.

"You bet. I was thinking she could come to the farm right after school. Then maybe you could pick her up on your way home from work. That way she'd have her evenings free for homework and any chores you might have for her."

Mom thought for a long time. Eventually she sighed. "Well, I guess we could give it a try. I just hope Kirsty makes herself useful. It's like pulling teeth at home to get her to tidy her room or wash the dishes."

"Thank you, Linda. I really appreciate this."

Kirsty hugged Lancelot's neck, grateful for the small reprieve.

12

For the next two weeks, Kirsty's life ran on a tight schedule. She rose early in the morning to bike to the farm and tend to Lancelot before school started. Everything took twice as long to do with only one useful hand. First she'd give the pony a flake of hay. While he munched his breakfast, she'd smear ointment on his cuts, take off his blanket, and give him a good grooming. Then Lucy would halter him so she could walk him around the yard for exercise while Faye quickly cleaned his stall and gave him fresh water and more hay. She'd have breakfast with the Marches in the kitchen of the old farmhouse before running down the driveway with Faye to catch the bus to school.

During the day, Lucy would top up the pony's water bucket, throw him more hay, give him his medication, and dab his cuts with ointment.

After school, Kirsty would go through the whole routine again – pick stall, treat wounds, groom, and walk while Faye worked her ponies. She'd stop Lancelot by the ring to watch Faye ride. The pony grazed the grass shooting up by the fence while Kirsty leaned on his shoulder, trying to seal every moment in her memory.

Sometimes when Kirsty's mom came to take her home, Lucy invited them to stay for supper. When the meal was done and the dishes washed up, the girls did their homework together at the big dining room table while the adults talked in the living room.

On the drive home through the chilly spring evening, Mom would ask about Lancelot. She'd listen as Kirsty gave her a progress report. At the end, Mom would nod and start to talk about something else.

After the first few days, the swelling left Lancelot's legs. The deep cuts slowly filled in with moist pink and yellow bumps. The veterinarian called it "granulating flesh." Kirsty thought it looked horrible, but Dr. Kelly, when he came to remove the stitches partway through the second week, said it was a natural part of the healing process.

Kirsty looked over her pony with a mixture of relief and despair. Lancelot was mending quickly. Tiny pink railway tracks crossed his chest and forearms where the sutures had been. The shaved hair was growing back and would soon cover the scars. The larger wounds were shrinking every day. Soon the pony would be well enough to be sold.

He had filled out over the past month, but even so, he was thin. His head looked too long and large at the end of his skinny neck, and his hip bones still jutted through his patchwork hide.

"Who's going to want him?" Kirsty burst out as Faye rode by one afternoon. "Lancelot's not fancy or well trained like your ponies. How's he going to get a good home?" Lancelot lifted his head and looked at her with his bright black eyes. Would anyone else recognize the intelligence glowing there?

"We'll find him one," Faye said stoutly, halting Robin beside them. "He won't go to anyone nasty."

Lancelot bumped Kirsty's hand, begging to be scratched under the chin. "Thanks," she mumbled.

Faye hopped off Robin and ran up his stirrups. "Listen, I didn't want to say anything, but a lady's coming to try him out tomorrow."

"So soon? He's not completely healed."

"She understands about that. She sounds really nice, Kirsty. She's looking for a pony for her daughter. Not a show pony, just something safe and kind."

"Oh. How old is the daughter?"

"Nearly thirteen."

"Just like me. Lucky girl. What time is she coming?"

"Around one. We'll be in school."

"I won't get to meet her."

"It'll just be the mom. It's supposed to be a surprise."

Kirsty's mouth tasted sour. Lucky, *lucky* girl, to be given a pony as a surprise. "I'd better put Lancelot back in his stall."

"Kirsty, I'm sorry," said Faye.

Kirsty shrugged off her friend's sympathy. Faye could be sorry all she wanted; she wasn't the one losing her pony. "Yeah, well, I'm sorry too."

"Maybe this lady won't buy him," said Faye. "Maybe nobody'll buy him. He'll just stay and you can keep helping here and your mom will forget about selling him."

"Yeah right," said Kirsty bitterly. "Like that's going to happen. Come on, Lancelot." Back in his stall, the pony rested his head on her shoulder. Kirsty took a deep breath of his salty scent, ignoring the hairs tickling her nose. "You behave tomorrow. Faye thinks this could be a good home for you, so don't mess up."

She rubbed her cheek against the pony's. What she really wanted to say was *Buck the woman off as soon as she gets on,* but what good would that do Lancelot? For his own sake he needed to behave well so the buyer would look past his bony frame and barbed wire scars and see a kind, dependable pony.

"How's that arm doing?" asked Lucy, coming into the barn.

Kirsty held it up, flexing her wrist. The splint had been removed a few days before. "Pretty good. It's a bit weak, but I can use it. I got the corrals picked out."

"Good girl. Your mom's here."

"Already? I've still got things to do."

"I'll finish your chores for you. Get going. Don't keep your mother waiting."

"You're sure quiet," said Mom on the drive home.

"What's up?"

"Someone's coming to try out Lancelot tomorrow," said Kirsty.

"Ah. How do you feel about that?"

"I hope it's a really good home. He deserves that." Kirsty choked back a sob.

"Oh honey. Kirsty. . . "

"Yeah?"

Mom sighed. "Nothing. So, do you have much homework tonight?"

"Just a little."

"Mmm."

They said nothing more for the rest of the drive.

Kirsty lay on the kitchen floor using Jet as a pillow. Mom stepped over her outstretched legs on her way to the stove.

"Honestly, Kirsty, can't you sit in a chair? I nearly tripped over you."

"Sorry. Hey!" Kirsty's head hit the floor as Jet lumbered to his feet, barking. Someone knocked at the back door. "I'll get it!"

She flung open the door. "Dad! Janice! What are you doing here?"

"Hey, kid." Dad wrapped her in a hug. "We've come for supper."

"You have?" Kirsty moved aside to let them through. "Does Mom know?"

"Of course I do," said Mom. "Why do you think I'm cooking so much food?"

For the first time Kirsty realized there were two huge pots simmering on the stove. She sniffed and recognized the aroma of her mother's homemade spaghetti sauce. At the counter, Mom was tearing lettuce and throwing it into a salad bowl. "Hi, Richard. Hi, Janice. And hello there, Brandon sweetie. Supper's just about ready. Kirsty, please set the table."

Janice kicked off her shoes and passed Brandon to Dad. "I'll give you a hand."

This is just too weird, thought Kirsty as they sat at the table eating their meal. Brandon smacked his spaghetti with the palm of his hand, splattering beads of red sauce on his bib. She looked over and saw Mom grinning at the toddler.

"So, Dad, why are you here?" Kirsty asked.

"To see you, of course."

"But it's not even the weekend."

"Well, we had some things to do in the area."

"What kind of things?"

Dad waggled his eyebrows above his glasses. "Oh, just things."

After supper, Janice and Dad did the dishes.

"That's my job," said Kirsty.

"We'll do them," Janice said. "It would be a big help if you could keep Brandon amused. His cars and trucks are in my bag."

The toddler rolled a tiny fire truck across the floor

toward Jet. He squealed with laughter as the old dog thumped his thick tail. Kirsty caught the child's wrist and stroked his hand along the Labrador's head and neck.

"Pet him nicely, that's a boy. No, don't hit him with your truck."

"Kirsty's so good with him," Janice murmured to Dad.

The toddler crouched on his haunches and stared gravely at Kirsty. She studied the apple-cheeked face with the round, hazel eyes and topping of pale, gold hair. This was her brother. Had she looked like him as a baby? He pushed his fire truck at her. She turned the toy around and rolled it back to him. The little boy grinned.

"Guess we'd better get going," said Janice, drying the last fork. "Brandon'll be a monster tomorrow if he doesn't get a good night's sleep."

"Are you here for the weekend?" asked Kirsty.

"You bet," said Dad. "How about we get together tomorrow after school?"

"I have to work at the farm. Lucy depends on me." As much as she wanted to spend time with her father, Kirsty had to know how things had gone with Lancelot.

"Sure, that's okay. We'll catch up with you there."

Brandon let out a mournful wail. He held out his arms. Janice scooped him up.

"Oh, you're one tired young fellow, aren't you? Will

you hold him for me while I put on my shoes and coat?" She held him out to Kirsty.

Kirsty held the toddler awkwardly. He stiffened, his eyes widening.

"Cuddle him, so he feels secure," said Mom.

Brandon's bottom lip trembled. Fat tears rolled from his eyes. He butted his head against Kirsty, muttering ominously.

Janice jammed toy trucks into her giant cotton bag. "Hang on, Brandon, I'm coming."

Kirsty grabbed the fire truck and held it up to him. "Look, Brandon, it's your truck."

Brandon batted the truck away.

"Here, let me have him." Mom plucked the child out of Kirsty's arms. She snuggled him up against her shoulder and rubbed his back. "Hush, little Brandon, that's a boy. Aren't you a darling?"

Brandon rubbed his eyes and let out a huge yawn.

Dad finished tying his shoe and stood up. Mom passed the toddler to him. "He's a beautiful child, Richard."

Dad smiled down at his sleepy son. He looked up at Kirsty, still smiling. "Thank you, Linda. Thank you very much."

Mom smiled back. "You're welcome."

13

By lunch hour the next day, Kirsty couldn't take it anymore.

"I'm going," she told Faye. She got up and tossed the remains of her pickle and cheese sandwich in the garbage.

ı "Huh?" mumbled Faye, chewing a mouthful of apple. "Hey, wait up." She ran after Kirsty out of the school.

Kirsty marched off the school grounds and onto the sidewalk.

"Where are we going?" asked Faye, trotting beside her.

"To the farm. I have to see what these people are like."

"What? We can't walk all that way!"

"I can."

"But what about school? Shouldn't we tell someone we're leaving?"

Kirsty shook her head. "They'll just try to stop us."

"There's going to be trouble," Faye predicted.

"You don't have to come."

"I know." With a heavy sigh, Faye quickened her pace to keep up with Kirsty.

The journey to the farm took forever on foot. Kirsty

tried to make time pass more quickly by pretending she was on Lancelot, prancing proudly along the street and out of town. She gave up when the sidewalk ran out. Now they were walking along the side of a country road.

"How long do you think this lady will take to try out Lancelot?" she puffed.

Faye shrugged. "Depends. One person will know right away. Another person will ride forever trying to make up her mind. Hey, slow down. I can't walk any faster."

Kirsty ignored her and pressed on. The road turned a corner and ran up a steep hill. Every step was like climbing a stair.

An empty dump truck rattled past heading downhill. Another dump truck grumbled up the hill, loaded with gravel. Kirsty and Faye veered onto a lawn to give the massive vehicle room. The truck roared by them and vanished around a bend in the road.

In tired silence the girls trudged along. The road levelled out and Kirsty's feet felt suddenly lighter. She looked up. The road to Hillcroft Farm was in sight. "Nearly there!"

"What's all that noise?" asked Faye.

In the distance, machinery thumped and banged and rumbled, the sounds growing louder as the girls moved on. They turned off the main road and stopped. The dump truck that had passed earlier trundled down the road, spewing gravel from its upturned box. Behind it, a huge, orange machine resembling an over-grown farm tractor chugged down the middle of the road.

A flagman came up to them. "Hey, you kids, get back out of the way!"

"We're going to Hillcroft Farm," said Kirsty.

The truck finished dumping the gravel. It rattled away to the main road. The orange machine screeched forward, its enormous blade flattening the gravel.

The flagman shook his yellow hard hat. "You can't go through while the grader's working. You'll have to wait."

"But we can't –"

Faye grabbed Kirsty's elbow and towed her away. "We'll cut through the neighbour's fields." She crawled through a fence and trotted across the grass. "Hurry up!"

Kirsty sprinted after her.

After squeezing through three more fencelines, they made it to a grove of trees above the barn. "There he is!" Kirsty pointed to Lancelot standing amidst a small crowd. "Who are all those people?" She could see three or four people gathered around the pony.

"I don't know. Lancelot's wearing his halter so he must have been ridden already. Let's get closer so we can hear what they're saying."

Kirsty followed as Faye picked her way through the underbrush. They came out against the backside of the barn. Off in the distance they could hear the relentless drone of heavy machinery working on the road. Quietly, they sidled up to the end of the barn.

". . . kept flinging his head," said a woman's voice. "He doesn't seem to be very well trained."

"That's Janice!" hissed Kirsty. "What's she doing here?"

"Shh!"

Yapping, Stubby charged around the corner. He squeaked with delight at finding Faye crouched against the barn wall.

"Hey, come back here!" said Dad.

Kirsty and Faye stiffened.

"Got you," he said, right around the corner. A high-pitched shriek filled the air. "No, you can't follow the puppy."

The shrieking receded. Kirsty peeked out. Dad was packing Brandon under his arm, walking back toward the little group gathered in front of the barn.

"What's going on?" whispered Faye.

"I don't understand. Janice and Dad are here and so is Mom. They're all talking with Lucy. I don't see anyone else."

"Maybe the buyer didn't show up. Or maybe. . . " Faye broke off.

"What?"

"Well, maybe she made an offer and Lucy's telling your family about it."

"Oh no!" Kirsty slid down the rough, wood wall, heedless of slivers.

"Don't get upset, Kirsty, you don't know for sure,"

said Faye. She peeked around the corner. "Look, your mom and Janice seem to be arguing about something."

Kirsty looked. Mom shook her head, arms crossed, while Janice gestured and talked. Dad wrestled a squirming Brandon and laughed at something Lucy said. He unclipped his cell phone and held it to his ear. Walking away from the others, he released Brandon and gave him a gentle push in the direction of his mother.

Lancelot towed Janice to a patch of grass in front of the barn. Carrying grooming tools and a bridle and saddle, Lucy and Mom went inside.

Brandon took a few steps toward his mother. He crouched down, poking at something on the ground. His round head came up like a pony's when it catches the rustle of hay at feeding time. He straightened and pointed his finger at the driveway.

"What's he doing?" asked Faye.

"He hears the machines working. He's crazy about trucks and big machines," explained Kirsty. "Uh-oh."

Brandon was moving toward the driveway. Janice leaned into the open door of the barn, calling to Lucy and Mom. Any moment now she was sure to turn around and see her tiny son scooting across the farmyard.

Janice bobbed her head and waved her free hand in the air to illustrate a point. Kirsty willed her to stop talking and look behind her.

Short legs pumping like pistons, Brandon reached the top of the driveway and kept going.

"Hey!" Kirsty stepped out from behind the barn. "Brandon!"

Janice whirled around. "Kirsty? What on earth are you doing here?"

"Brandon! He's running down the driveway!"

Janice caught a glimpse of the toddler's red T-shirt before he was hidden by the trees. "Brandon!" She dropped Lancelot's lead rope and ran after her child.

"Brandon! Come back," shouted Dad from the far end of the yard.

"The trucks!" said Faye. "What if the drivers don't see him?"

Kirsty whistled. Lancelot flung up his head. She whistled again and the pony trotted to her. "Good boy," she breathed. "Quick, Faye."

Faye caught her ankle and boosted her up onto the pony's back. Kirsty slammed her heels into his sides. Lancelot shot forward.

"Look out," she screeched. The adults scattered as they galloped through them, the pony's hooves ringing out like gunshots.

She caught a flicker of bright red amidst the dark trunks of the old trees. Digging her hands into his mane, she urged Lancelot on. They rounded a slight bend and ahead, she could see Brandon, his sturdy little legs propelling him over the ground faster than anyone could have imagined. Over the drumbeat of

Lancelot's hoofs, Kirsty could hear the screech and groan of heavy machinery.

Brandon had nearly reached the road. Kirsty bent low over the pony's neck. She chirped and he stretched out his stride. A shadow darkened the end of the driveway. A shrill beeping began as a huge dump truck backed up.

"Brandon!" screamed Kirsty. The driver would never see him in time.

The toddler slowed, his head tilted up to gape at the truck towering above him. It was going to be okay, Kirsty realized. He would stop before he got to the road.

And then she saw the tailgate of the truck turn toward them. The dump truck was backing into the driveway. Brandon froze as the enormous tires rolled slowly toward him.

Lancelot jerked to a halt beneath her. His head swung up. His body began to twist away from the rattling contraption lumbering in their direction. Above the rumble of the engine and the clanging of the empty metal box she heard Brandon's shrill wail of terror.

"Come on!" Kirsty dug her heels into Lancelot. She felt him hesitate, then leap forward. They were alongside Brandon, then in front, swinging sideways across the driveway between him and the dump truck. Kirsty leaned back, pulling on the lead rope. "Whoa!"

Lancelot shook his head at the pressure. His hindquarters lowered and he skidded to a halt. Abruptly, the dump truck stopped too, its engine growling. Lancelot trembled, his ears flicking nervously. "Steady now," Kirsty said.

She slid down the pony's side and snatched up Brandon. The startled little boy burst into loud sobs.

"Shh, it's okay, Brandon," she said. She hugged his stocky body tightly to her, rubbing her face against his silky head. "Everything's all right, little brother."

"Kid, are you crazy?" The truck driver scrambled down from the cab. "You nearly ran right into me! What's the matter with you?"

Kirsty burst into tears along with Brandon.

"Brandon! Kirsty!" Janice seized the toddler from Kirsty.

"Is he okay?" called Dad, close behind. "Kirsty, what's wrong? Did the truck hit you or Brandon?"

Kirsty shook her head, unable to stop the tears.

Then Mom was there, wrapping her arms around Kirsty and stroking her hair. "Are you hurt, Kirsty? Did you fall off?"

"No." She buried her face in her mother's shoulder. "I'm okay."

Mom hugged her fiercely. "How's Brandon?" she asked over Kirsty's head.

"He's okay, Linda," answered Janice. "Just scared."

"Oh, thank goodness."

Kirsty lifted her head. Faye had taken Lancelot's lead rope and was checking him over. "He's fine," she told Kirsty. "He was amazing. So were you."

Lucy spoke to the truck driver. Moments later he climbed in the cab of his truck and drove off.

"Thank you, Kirsty," said Janice. "We would never have reached Brandon in time. You were very brave."

"It was Lancelot. He was scared of the truck but he went right between it and Brandon." She swallowed. "He did it because I asked him to."

"What a good pony you are," said Faye, rubbing Lancelot's forehead.

"You were both very brave," said Mom.

"I didn't know you could ride like that," said Dad. "Not even a saddle or a bridle."

"Or a helmet," said Lucy dryly.

"I didn't think. . . again," Kirsty admitted.

"Well, this was an emergency. Just remember to wear it next time you ride."

"Sure." Kirsty didn't bother to remind her she wouldn't be riding anymore.

"Kirsty!" said Mom. "What *are* you doing here? Why aren't you in school?"

"Oh boy," muttered Faye.

"We skipped out. It's not Faye's fault. I made her come," Kirsty told Lucy.

"Skipped out? But why?" asked Dad.

Kirsty felt a puff of warm air on her cheek. Lancelot rested his head on her shoulder. "I wanted to meet her and see what she's like."

"Meet *who*?"

"The lady who's going to buy Lancelot."

The adults were all trying very hard not to look at each other. Kirsty's heart sank. It was true. Lancelot had been sold.

"Hmm, I see," said Mom. "How did you get here? You didn't hitchhike, did you?"

"We walked."

"You walked all the way from town? That's miles."

Kirsty shrugged. "Well, I'd better put Lancelot away." She led the pony back up the driveway.

Faye hurried after her. "You know, I was thinking – maybe you can still come and ride with me, even after. . . I'll ask Lucy if you want."

"Thanks, Faye, but not right now. I can't even think about riding another pony. Maybe some day."

"I know what you mean. I'd feel the same way about Robin."

Above the clopping of Lancelot's hooves they heard the rise and fall of the adults' voices behind them. Kirsty tried to close her ears against the sounds. She did not want to hear any of the details about the sale of her beloved pony.

"My mind's made up," said Janice shrilly. "I think we should do it."

Lancelot pulled the cotton rope through Kirsty's limp fingers, heading for the green grass by the barn. She scurried after him and tugged him away.

"Kirsty, wait there a moment," called Dad. "We've got something to tell you."

"No, Dad, please. Not right now. I just can't. . ."
Kirsty yanked on the rope, but Lancelot dragged his
toes, reluctant to leave the grass behind.

"Kirsty!" cried Mom.

Lucy set her hand lightly on Kirsty's shoulder. "Girl,
listen to what your folks have to say."

14

Squaring her shoulders, Kirsty turned back.

Janice looked at Dad. Both of them nodded to Mom.

"Okay," said Mom, taking a deep breath. "Kirsty, we've been doing a lot of talking the last little while, that is Janice and your father and me. And. . . "

Kirsty twined her fingers through Lancelot's bushy mane, wondering why her mother had to drag it out like this. Didn't she realize how much it was hurting Kirsty to have her pony sold? Didn't she care?

"Well, we still feel, and I want to be clear on this, that the *way* you went about getting this pony and then concealing him from us was completely and utterly wrong."

Kirsty couldn't take any more. "I know, Mom. That's why you've sold him. I understand all this. Now can I just put him away?"

"No, Kirsty, he hasn't been sold. And he's not going to be."

Kirsty stared at her fingers tangled in the pony's mane. She lifted her eyes and saw a look of joy on Faye's face. "Is this a joke?"

Mom grinned. "Oh, you're always so suspicious, just like your –" She glanced over at Kirsty's father. "No, dear, we mean it."

"But I thought we couldn't afford to keep a pony."

"Well, money *is* always in short supply, but we're all going to pitch in. And Lucy's come up with a special arrangement."

"What do you mean?" Kirsty turned to Lucy.

"Well, I couldn't see losing my chore girl, not after all the work I've put into training her." Lucy chuckled at her own humour. "We figured you wouldn't mind continuing with some of the chores you've been doing – picking corrals, cleaning tack, grooming ponies – to help pay for your pony's board. Of course, you're going to have a couple of lessons a week as well."

"You mean Lancelot's going to stay here? And I'm going to have riding lessons too?"

"That's great!" said Faye. "We'll be able to ride together every day!"

"I've still got my old saddle and bridle," said Janice. "I'll let you have them, if you want."

"Oh, yes, please." A saddle and bridle too! It was too much to take in.

"Then we'll bring them with us when we come to see you again," said Dad. "Can you wait a couple of weeks?"

Nodding, Kirsty sagged against Lancelot's neck, overcome by the sudden turn of events. This was more than she could have ever dared imagine.

"Honey, is everything all right?" asked Mom anxiously.

"Yes, Mom, everything's wonderful! You'll let that lady know that he's not for sale anymore, won't you?"

"What lady?"

"The one who tried him out today."

"Oh, *that* lady," said Dad. He rubbed his chin. "I don't know, Kirsty, she seemed to like him a lot. What if she offers a good price for him?"

"Richard, don't tease Kirsty," scolded Janice. "*I* was the lady who rode Lancelot."

"*You?* But why?"

"Because I'm the only one with any riding experience. We wanted to be sure he's a reliable pony for you. And he certainly proved that."

"Thank you, Janice."

Janice tipped her head. "Any time, Kirsty."

Mom cautiously patted Lancelot's shoulder.

"Hey, Mom, would you like to ride him?" asked Kirsty.

"Who, me?" She stepped back hastily. "Oh no, I don't think so."

Dad stood alongside Lancelot, Brandon clinging to his neck, monkey-style.

"See the nice pony, son? Can you say pony? Pony."

Brandon pursed his lips, making puffing sounds. "Poh." He grinned and repeated the sound over and over. "Poh, poh, poh." Stretching his arms to Lancelot, he wriggled frantically.

"You want to pet the pony?" Dad stroked Lancelot's neck. "Isn't he nice and soft?"

Brandon reached out and latched onto a fistful of mane. Bracing his legs on Dad's chest, he squirmed out of his arms and onto the pony's back. Sprawled on top of Lancelot he chortled merrily. The pony took a step and he crowed with delight at the swaying motion.

Lucy quirked her mouth at the sight of Dad and Janice trying to persuade Brandon to come off Lancelot. "Looks like there's another rider in the family. Guess you'll be teaching him one day."

"Guess so," agreed Kirsty. She reached up and gently moved her brother's legs forward so he could sit up. "That's better, hey, Brandon?"

Her brother ducked his chin in agreement.

15

Kirsty checked the notice board beside the tack room for her list of afternoon chores.

Tack room, pick corrals, sweep barn floor.

Tack room? What about the tack room? Usually Lucy was more specific. Was she supposed to sweep and wash the floor? Or clean some tack? Kirsty looked at the walls of saddles and bridles with dismay, worried she was expected to clean all of them in one afternoon. She wouldn't have time to ride Lancelot if she had to saddle soap and oil every single bridle and saddle.

Then she noticed a saddle stand in the middle of the crowded room. A lustrous chocolate-brown saddle sat on it, with a matching snaffle bridle draped over the seat. She looked back at the saddle racks on the wall. Not one of them was empty. Kirsty's heart gave a funny little skip. She walked over to the saddle on the stand and stroked her hand over the smooth leather. Her fingers felt the edge of a metal plate on the back of the cantle. She tipped up the saddle on its pommel and read the engraving on the tiny brass plaque. *Kirsty Hagen.*

"So you found it," said Lucy from the door. Stubby wriggled past to snuffle Kirsty's boots.

"This is mine?" whispered Kirsty.

"That's why your name's on it. The bridle's yours too."

"Oh!" Kirsty's eyes lit up with surprise and delight.

"Your folks dropped them off earlier. Said they'll come back later. Oh, and your mom brought this." Lucy picked up a small cardboard box off the old chair.

Kirsty stared at the picture on the box. "Is this really—"

"Open it and see."

She lifted the lid and pulled out a black riding helmet. "For me?"

Lucy took the helmet and set it on Kirsty's head. "Fits good. Here, buckle that chinstrap up nice and snug."

Faye and Robin poked their heads in the door. "Lucy, can we jump today? Hey, Kirsty, did you get a new hard hat?"

Kirsty nodded. She stepped aside to give Faye a clear view of the saddle stand.

Faye blinked. "You got your saddle and bridle!"

"We'd better make sure this new gear fits your pony," said Lucy. "Bring him in the barn."

"What about my chores?" asked Kirsty.

"You can do them later, after riding."

"But I might not get everything done before Mom picks me up."

Lucy waggled her sandy brows. "Oh, something tells me you're going to have some help with the chores. You know the old saying: Many hands make light work. Now go catch that pony."

Snatching a carrot from the feed room, Kirsty hurried across the yard, a halter flung over her shoulder. She whistled. From his hillside pasture, Lancelot whinnied. He burst out of the trees, galloping down the grassy slopes with his tail flying behind like a banner. A trio of ponies followed – silver, russet, and golden shadows. They slid up to the fence, tossing their thick manes and stamping their tiny hooves.

Lancelot stood still. He held his head high, bright black eyes fixed on Kirsty. She slipped through the fence and buckled on the halter, feeding him bits of carrot. The younger ponies kept back as Kirsty and Lancelot went out the gate.

Down at the barn, Stubby began to yap. A silver car bumped slowly up the potholed driveway. Behind it chugged a little blue car.

Kirsty grinned and waved at the cars. "Everyone's coming to see us ride in our new saddle and bridle," she told Lancelot. He shook his bushy mane and nudged her hand for more carrot.

Abruptly he halted, his ears snapped forward. In the ring, Faye trotted Robin toward a line of jumps. The bay pony bounced up and down over the fences like a rubber ball. Lucy shouted encouragement as they cantered at the stone wall in the middle of the ring. Robin's black hooves thudded in the sand, shooting up little puffs of dust. His quarters dropped down to a crouch and he raised his neck high. He pushed off into the air, soaring over the huge obstacle. Faye whooped with joy and Lucy laughed.

Robin touched down and kicked up his heels.

Kirsty placed a hand on her pony's checkered neck. Lancelot quivered with excitement.

Jumping? Kirsty caught her breath. In her head she could see herself on Lancelot, leaping over jumps as high as his chest. She could feel the sting of his mane on her chin, the squeeze of her helmet, the rub of the stirrup irons on her boots.

Why not? Anything was possible, she knew that. She had a pony and a saddle and bridle, a place to keep him, and new friends. They could learn to jump. Lucy would teach her for sure.

Lancelot chuffed, pawing the ground. "Soon, Lancelot, soon," she murmured.

At the barn, car doors slammed. Brandon squealed at the sight of ponies all around. Voices called her name.

"Come on, Lancelot." Her pony trotting beside her, Kirsty ran to meet her family.

About the Author

JULIE WHITE started making up horse stories at a young age after her parents told her she couldn't keep a pony in the backyard of their Vancouver home. When she was twelve, her family moved onto a farm near Vernon in the interior of British Columbia, and she got her first horse, a headstrong chestnut named Roger.

Julie lives on a horse farm in Armstrong with her husband, Robert, a former jockey, where they raise thoroughbreds for racing and jumping. She rides every day and competes in jumping classes at horse shows, often against her two grown daughters. She's a Pony Club examiner, riding instructor and course designer. This is Julie's first book.